Names, characters, events and incidents are the products of the author's imagination. Any resemblance to actual persons, living or dead, or actual events is purely coincidental. ... This novel's story and characters are fictitious

There is an exception to this rule; The names of the Flannery Family are used with their permission as is that of Mr.Joseph Armstrong, good friends who are honored here.

On the Cover

I have to take a moment and thank George Jenkins and his staff at the Eagles Mere Air Museum. Special thanks to Karen Heisman for her efforts in coordinating our request. They graciously allowed our photo shoot with the last remaining flying example of an Alexander Eaglerock A-4 biplane.

The town of Eagles Mere is known as the town that time forgot, a very fitting title for a town that hosts one of the finest air museums I have ever seen. Mr. Jenkins' aviation museum is focused upon the Golden Age of Aviation a period from 1908 to 1940. It is a flying museum where you just may witness the spectacular sight of a vintage aircraft alive over the rolling Pennsylvania hills. It is nothing less than amazing with a large portion of the aircraft displayed being the last remaining flying examples of that particular model.

It pains me that we are using a black and white photo to maintain a certain vintage flavor on our cover. It works for the book. It however, does no justice to the beautiful aircraft displayed behind our models.

I have to petition you to please go to:
"www.eaglesmereairmuseum.org" Please take a moment and browse their website, or better yet visit them at Merritt Field Airport, 100 Merritt Field Rd. Laporte, PA 18626. (The airfield is named after George's son Merritt). Hours of operation are available on the website as is a phone number and the opportunity to preview the pictures of what is beyond a

shadow of a doubt a pristine collection of aircraft and motors from the period. The website calls it Pennsylvania's finest air attraction. I wholeheartedly agree with that assessment. It's truly spectacular! I have to mention that the museum is also focused on the great women of aviation from that period as well, daring young ladies whose courage and dedication helped to form the foundation of an industry and a sport still in its infancy. Make the trip and travel back in time with the Eagles Mere Air Museum.

One more quick moment of gratitude: Thank you to our models Patrick Newhart and Kate Donithen for bringing my characters to life.

TIMELESS

A Novel by
Mike Rencavage

For Judi

I love you Belle

Prologue

There are few men who have influenced my life as greatly as my grandfather. He was always there for me, his strong hands guiding me along. I can still hear the gentle tone of his voice offering encouragement and praise as the tiniest of personal victories were transformed into magnificent accomplishments.

He was a delight, a man of passion and conviction, a man of honor. These characteristics are often related to stern, quiet men. To meet him was to realize that stern was only one part of the equation and quiet most certainly had little to do with it. He had an inner strength hidden in the layers of a loving, caring individual who wanted nothing more than to appreciate his every day. He would take great pleasure in sharing with you the joy he found in being alive on this planet for as long as he had been and living the adventure that was his life. Grandpa was a character: larger than life, an icon in my mind's eye. He was my own personal superhero.

He stood only five feet, eight inches tall, but to his dying day he was physically fit, lean and muscular. Our weekly hikes together along the waterfalls at Ricketts Glen State Park showed his stamina and the ingenuity he demonstrated in handling every situation that arose in life reminded me of a sort of real-world Indiana Jones. He even wore his leather jacket in all but the summer months. There was no fedora in his wardrobe. Above all else, though, it was his charm and intrigue, his robust presentation of life, that defined him.

I will never forget him or the lessons he shared with me. His life lessons were often shared in tales of his past epic adventures. He was a great storyteller. Had his words been written and his passion and depth of insight been recorded on the pages of a book, it would no doubt have topped the New York Times Bestsellers list and shared the magic of the man he was with all the world for generations to come. He was a man who could spin a yarn and keep you captivated from start to finish. His tales were often based in truth, but his embellishments entertained and amused us. We never minded the fact that we could be with him during an adventure, and his version of it was always far more interesting than our memory.

The pages of this book are taken from his own personal journal, given to me in response to a simple question the evening after my grandmother's funeral on January 10th , 1993, a terribly sad day for every member of our family. We all loved her. She was our matriarch. The moment he placed this journal in my hands was one of the rare occasions that tears had fallen from my grandfather's loving eyes and his smile had vanished into the darkness of the night, dimming, but not extinguishing, the light that shined within the man.

The dates don't seem to make sense at first, but in the end it all came together for me in *his legendary style. The truth is within these pages, though as with his storytelling I am sure that many embellishments have been injected over the years into the tale of how my grandfather met his soulmate. Facts usually mixed quite well with fiction for him. I offer now the incredible story as he had written it himself, in the pages of a journal not intended for anyone except his family, but sure to be touching to the hearts of those that will listen to the final tale my grandfather shared with me.*

Christopher Nevin

JOURNAL

Journal Entries

Property of

Michael Joseph Nevin

2102 Pittston Avenue

Scranton, PA 18505

December 27th, 1987

This is my first entry in the new journal. In the past, my life has been chronicled for the members of my family in much the same manner as this, leaving the legacy of my joys and pains and the lessons I've learned on the pages of my journals in the form of sequential daily entries. It has been almost ritualistic to me. It is a chance for me to share with my children and grandchildren who I strove with all my might to be. Today's entry is different, however; it is more of a story.

The events took place in a different time and the story is being shared as one entry to preserve the memory of how I met my wife, the woman that I believe was my soulmate. She was, in fact, destined to be with me, no matter what time or place we came from. She is the love of my life, and as I sit here writing, she sleeps in the bed beside me. She sleeps comfortably, undisturbed by my scribbling. As I look upon her picture, the very picture from the story I am about to share, her beauty intoxicates me. Yes, we have grown old together, but each day, she is to me that beautiful young woman with the most amazing eyes I have ever seen. I want my family to know the story of how I came to be with her. It wasn't an easy road, but these things rarely are.

It was Saturday, August 4th, 1993. (Please take note of the fact that I was only 27 years old on that specific date, a date that resides in my personal past, but at the time of this writing on December 27th, 1987 is yet to come around again. Time travel is tricky that way.) So, like I said, my story begins on that fateful day, Saturday, August 4th, 1993. It all started as a normal Saturday morning. We were having coffee at the breakfast nook, just me and Rocky, my peaceful labrador retriever pup. It was our daily routine. I sat and sipped my morning brew while Rocky enjoyed a petting of his belly curled up on the booth like cushion beneath the kitchen window.

There was a knock on my front door, a rapid, aggressive knock that startled me at first, then angered me, when I spilled my coffee down my pant leg. I walked to the door and opened it only to find that no one was there—not a soul.

I went to the street. There was nothing to be seen, not even a sprinting teenager in the distance. I turned to head back to the kitchen and plastered on my door was a handwritten note in big letters with a simple statement.

Open your mind,

trust your heart.

What a strange statement. To the best of my knowledge, there were no new-age gurus running around, taping bits of personal philosophies to the doors of strangers. It was so bizarre that I just grabbed it from the door and took it inside, tossing it on the table and not giving it more than a passing glance for the rest of the day.

The rest of the day was quite normal for me. I started by taking a morning class with my Tang Soo Do instructor, followed by a short trip to the airport to change the oil in my old Stearman biplane and have some lunch with a few of my flying buddies. Then I headed back to the house to cut the grass and chop some wood before settling in for the evening. These were routines in my life, aside from the wood chopping in August, but a strong cold front had passed and the evening was forecast to drop into the 40s. The fire would be a welcome respite in the cold, evening hours.

Since the passing of my parents the previous month, it had been just my dog and me. Twenty-seven years old and still single. My love life had suffered as a result of building my career as an aviator and the time spent taking care of my parents in their waning years. I was not opposed to the traditional family and marriage. With all of the time and effort I had spent in becoming a pilot and any spare time being spent at the nursing home, there just wasn't much time for dating, and as a result I hadn't met the right person yet. I knew she was out there somewhere, the one who would stir me up and turn me inside out—my soulmate. Every so often, I would lose my faith and doubt her existence, but somehow, I always came back to my belief in the concept of a soulmate. I always held true to the idea that the love of your life has to possess that deep, passionate feeling that lets you know that you are meant for each other and that you will go to the ends of Earth for your partner. That's what I was thinking about as I drifted off to sleep in front of the fire that evening.

Chapter 1

I wasn't startled awake; no, I simply opened my eyes and the dream world vanished as I returned to reality. With the soft glow of the last remaining embers still crackling in the fireplace, I sat up slowly, then stood and collected my blanket and pillow from the sofa. It was then, at that moment, that stitch in time, that was the beginning of this story. It may sound incredible, perhaps even untrue, but truth is often stranger than fiction. It has been 60 years since that moment and I still cannot bring into reason every aspect in this chain of events; perhaps you will have a greater understanding than I. For me, the spirit of the story was enough. I never felt the need to spend a great deal of time trying to understand all that had happened to me or to return to my life prior to that moment. I was simply happy—contented—having found what mattered most to me. There was one key element that happened prior to that moment: the note. Its simple message kept ringing through as my reality began to shift before my eyes.

When I turned back around, my intent was to simply spread the embers and let the glimmer fade to darkness, then head on up to bed. That never happened, for in that moment, that precious split second, I saw her. She wasn't a ghost or some devilish spirit conjured up by a restless mind. She was real. I gazed in disbelief at her standing in the doorway. I was captivated by her beauty. I was breathless, unable to speak, and in my silence, I fell in love.

She stood and looked at me, as surprised to see me as I was to see her. Her long, strawberry-blonde hair flowed elegantly over her shoulders. Her eyes, the most amazing eyes I had ever seen, were as blue as the Caribbean Sea. In those eyes I saw all that she was: beautiful, kind, loving, passionate. In that momentary glimpse, I felt as though I had seen through to her very soul. She smiled; shyly, I smiled back. Then she turned as if to walk toward the stairs and disappeared. She vanished into thin air! I stood there for a few seconds recalling the curve of her face, the pattern of her dress, that smile, those eyes. Her beauty had completely enchanted me. I never so much as uttered a single word, not one, nor did she. What I remember most was what I felt: a peaceful loving kindness, a sense of belonging that I had never felt before in all of my 27 years.

I shook my head and rubbed my eyes, not knowing what I had seen. I went to look for her throughout the house, but she was gone. I was seriously starting to doubt my sanity. I may not have known what I had seen, but I knew what I had felt. What I sensed in that moment was emblazoned upon my heart forever.

After some restless tossing and turning and the occasional scan of my room with hopes of seeing her face once more, I finally fell asleep. The next thing I knew, the sun was beaming through the skylight, annoying me into the slightly-awakened grogginess of the morning. But it was barely morning. The alarm clock showed 11:00am and the time startled me. I had slept through my morning workout and would have to hustle to the airport if I was going to depart on time. My hurrying pushed the thoughts of my apparition to the back of my mind and I rushed myself along to make up for my little sleep-in.

That day was the day I had planned to fly my open cockpit biplane to Virginia to spend the rest of my vacation with my friend Bob and his wife Donna. I had been looking forward to the trip for quite some time and to the sailing we planned to do on the Chesapeake Bay. We would set sail by evening, provided the weather held out. Putting first things first, it was the flight to Virginia that I was concerned with.

The weather at my point of departure and at my destination was fine. It was the enroute weather that had me raising my eyebrows. Thunderstorms pocked my route of flight from just south of Lancaster, PA on into northern Virginia. Thunderstorms and antique biplanes don't really belong together.

The radar was showing widely scattered storms that were forecast to remain widely scattered throughout the afternoon. I felt certain that, with a bit of diligence and enough fuel onboard, I could circumnavigate the storms with enough room to keep myself both safe and comfortable.

I said goodbye to my friend Jimmy, a friend of mine for years, who was standing alongside one of the flight school Cessnas he owned. He was diligently replacing a bad magneto on the little airplane as I made my way through the main hangar and onto the ramp. I then grabbed my weather information, my maps and my backpack and climbed up on the lower wing of the Stearman. I placed everything in its appropriate spot and was ready to fly off for another adventure in the air. I just didn't realize how different this particular adventure would be.

I sat there in my cockpit with the sun glinting off the meticulously-polished white fabric of the lower wing and scanned the instruments, checking that everything was exactly as it should be in the first moments after engine start. The oil pressure was good, the oil temperature was rising, and the engine was rumbling along smoothly at just over 1100 revolutions per minute. The big oak control stick felt strong and solid in my hand. With such a wide cockpit, the old Stearman really had a roomy, comfortable feel to it.

The airplane was eighteen years older than I was, yet it looked like the day it rolled off the factory assembly line. That's the way it was when I bought it and that's the way I kept it as well. Everything was perfectly restored and perfectly maintained. There was only one minor flaw on the entire airplane, but I seemed to notice it every time I climbed in to go flying: on the lower right corner of the instrument panel was a small rectangular area that was slightly discolored. In its center were the remnants of some sort of adhesive tape. I had asked Joe Armstrong, the gentleman who had restored the airplane and flown it for years before selling it to me, what it was that had caused the mark. He just smiled and pointed to his wife.

He said the love of his life had accompanied him on every flight that airplane had ever made. She was not always there in person, though; her picture was stuck to that instrument panel from the day he brought the old airplane back to life. They had shared in every airborne adventure from one end of the country to the other. It was such a pure and romantic notion that it struck a chord with me and I had never tried to get rid of the mark her photo had left, partly out of respect for their love, and partly in the hopes that one day I could replace it with a picture that held the same meaning to me. My apparition from the previous evening tugged on my heart and I sat back in the cockpit for a second, thinking of her, without a clue as to where the love of my life was or if she even existed. Was my soulmate an honest-to-goodness living, breathing human being out there searching for me as I searched for her? Or was I destined to chase after mere visions in the night, apparitions that appear as the firelight fades to darkness?

Chapter 2

The biplane and I chugged along, enduring the gentle bumps of the afternoon sky just a thousand feet above the sun-soaked river that guided us from Wilkes-Barre all the way to Harrisburg, Pennsylvania. Over Harrisburg, the push of a button on the navigation receiver transformed me from a barnstorming flying ace to a commercial aviator following invisible radio waves from one point to the next at nowhere near breakneck speeds. The navigation radio may have made me more precise, but it did nothing to help me go any faster.

A few minutes later, I was on the ground at the Thomasville Airport in York, the last stop in my home state. In less than half an hour I had refueled the airplane, checked the weather, grabbed a quick sandwich and started on my way. I accelerated down the runway and raised the tail of the old biplane. I felt it then, a strange stumble in the motor. The plane that had shared so many adventures with me felt different, as if somehow, that collection of wood and fabric had sensed what was to come and was trying to warn me. I remember thinking how odd it felt.

The thought was intense, but it was brief, and in no time, things were normal again.

I could see a few thunderstorms building toward the horizon, they were along my path, but appeared to be far enough apart to allow me to pass without much concern. I pressed on, enjoying flying just for the fun of it as I headed off across Maryland with the sun on my wings, miles from any danger.

Not ten minutes after those stolen moments of peaceful bliss in the air..............

CRACK! The turbulence slammed me hard into my seat. Crack! I struggled to hold my altitude with the control stick shuddering in my hand as lightning bolts blazed toward the ground from roiling dark storm clouds to my left and right. I aimed toward a gap in the clouds, and within seconds of my passage, the gap was gone. The energy from the storms fed each other, creating a solid wall of airplane-splintering turbulence encased in darkness that spewed rain and shot lightning rapid-fire in all directions behind me. Ahead and to my right I saw my salvation, another gap in the storm clouds. I headed full speed toward the opening, hoping to slip through the gauntlet yet again unharmed. The scattered storms had banded together into lines of fierce billowing clouds, one upon another, energy feeding energy. My gap, my light at the end of tunnel, had disappeared completely and I was trapped.

Everywhere I looked were storms, lightning, rain. A sinking feeling came over me with so many thoughts racing through my head. I was lost for a moment in disbelief that I had ever allowed myself to get into that situation in that little airplane. I snapped myself out of it. I had to find a way. I knew the rule: never give up; fly it until it just won't fly anymore. I looked in every direction, hoping for an opening, a soft bright area, anything, any way out. I was flying in a small, clear area in the center of a group of storms. It was almost like being in the calm air in the center of a hurricane. I kept circling and looking for options as I talked myself to a state of calm that slowed my racing heart.

I remember mumbling to myself, *Keep your cool now*, as I scoured the earth below for an airport or even a farmer's field that was long and smooth enough for me to set down in. But then, at my darkest moment, with all hope waning, it appeared out of nowhere like a mirage in the desert. The bright-orange windsock flapped wildly in the breeze, indicating my prayers had been answered and I had found my salvation in the windblown grass of someone's private airstrip. It wasn't on the charts, but there it was as plain as day. The field was at least 3,000 feet long of soft, mowed grass. It was more of an old-time aerodrome than a runway, a large, clear square of earth with a windsock in the middle of the field. The aerodrome design would allow me to land into the wind no matter which direction it was coming from.

It was a tailwheel pilot's dream that appeared just in time to save me from a nightmare.
With lightning bolts exploding from every direction and the wind howling through the trees, I wrestled my little biplane toward the ground. Mixture full rich, throttle to idle, and a steep, banked glide to the left brought me quickly to the gentle rumble of my tires across the freshly-mowed grass. I gave a blast of throttle to taxi before the biplane and I came to rest in front of an old hangar.

The steel was rusted, the doors were blown off, and there was a hole in the roof that I could see from the distance of my cockpit. I wanted my pristine antique far from that decrepit artifact of a shelter. I ended up across the field driving my temporary tie-downs into the ground and securing the Stearman firmly to the earth. With the cockpit covers on, I reached into the baggage compartment for my flight bag and rustled around a bit to try and score some lunch. I ended up with a breakfast bar and a bottle of water, a weekend warrior's answer to a grumbling stomach. It was not a meal fit for a king, but it was food and it was the only option I had. Just as I opened the bottle to take a sip, the sky opened up above me, dumping rain on me in sheets, pelting me with raindrops the size of quarters. I ran toward that old hangar with my flight bag in hand. I made a dash that would make Jesse Owens proud. I was cold and tired—no, exhausted—from my recent battle with Mother Nature, and I was hungry too! What an afternoon.

Looking into the hangar from the outside, it was a mess. Old, rusting farm equipment filled the entire left side, a huge pile of wood lay rotting to the right. Whoever owned that place probably hadn't seen it for a very long time.

Nonetheless, it was keeping me out of the rain. I made my way over to sit against the tire of an old tractor, then I tore open the breakfast bar for a quick lunch. I watched in relative comfort as the storms blew fiercely across the field, and I waited patiently, looking into the distance in awe of the power of the storm.

I remember feeling this nagging chill that I just couldn't seem to shake. My dampened clothes were not helping matters, either. Suddenly, it came to me that it just might be a good time to start a little campfire. I had a small pocket knife and a magnesium stick in my flight bag. Looking over at the pile of dried-out wood and a few old newspapers, I knew I could warm things up in a hurry and maybe dry my clothes in the process. It seemed like a good plan, and I didn't have anything better to do with my spare time. I used a broken, old shovel to dig a pit far from the tractor and the pile of dried wood. I laid the old newspaper in the base of the pit, then headed off across the hangar to gather some appropriate pieces of wood from the pile. Climbing to the top of the neatly-stacked wood pile, I gathered a few old two-by-fours that showed promise. Lying across the top of the pile, I started to toss the wood to the ground in the direction of my fire pit. It all seemed to be coming together quite nicely and I would soon be sitting comfortably by the glow of a fire as the storm raged past outside.

The fire glowed in my mind as I gathered enough wood for a whole day's worth of burning. I was just about ready to dismount the wood pile and return to the hangar floor when I spied an old, wooden propeller off in the upper right corner of the pile. I thought about it for half of a second, then I scrambled up to take a look.

It was just about in my grasp. I stretched my arm as far as I could, but my fingertips remained about an inch shy of the prop. Sliding up the pile just a little bit further, I tried again when everything started to wobble. My right foot slipped away first, then my left, and my entire body fell backwards as my outstretched arm reached for my treasure. I scraped against wood and the occasional nail, bouncing and dropping my way to the backside of the wood pile. Sitting in pain on the dirt floor, I was just catching my breath when something startled me. A creature of some sort was rustling in the corner and I turned to look into the darkness, then I clicked on my little keychain flashlight. My heart rate finally settled at the sight of a mouse scurrying across the floor.

I saw the tail section first, then I grabbed the old tarp and, like a child unwrapping a Christmas present, I unveiled an amazing find. There in that decrepit old hangar, behind a pile of rotting wood, was a truly spectacular discovery. Beneath that tarp, for what had to be ages, was a rather well-preserved 1920's Alexander Eaglerock Biplane. Built to replace the aging postwar aircraft of its time the Eaglerock was a fantastic example of the golden age of aviation. The great ancestor of my beloved two-winger, it was a staple of aviation history. They had been everything from business transports to barnstorming airplanes that introduced the world to the wonders of flight, one small town fair at a time. Prior to that moment, I had only seen them at museums. The Eaglerock was an extremely rare airplane and this one was just sitting there wasting away, turned over to the sands of time.

I quickly but cautiously crawled into the cockpit. It was amazing. The cockpit was in remarkably good shape. I placed my right hand on the control stick, my left hand on the throttle and felt the history of the little plane in the palms of my hands. I was excited, to say the least. I took my trusty little light and scanned the sparse but effective cockpit.

Hmm, I thought, *that's funny*! There, in the lower right corner of the cockpit, right where the discoloration and the tape would be in my airplane, was an old photo. I remember thinking that it must be some sort of old aviator tradition or something, you know, to keep a picture of your girl with you at all times as a sort of good-luck charm. I reached over and removed the picture for a closer look.

The photo was black and white and the image had faded around the edges, but the beautiful woman that was captured that moment, all those years ago, shined through as plain as day. The sight of her startled me at first, then it sent shivers down my spine as I sat there studying the photo. It was her! The curve of her face, the pattern on her dress, those eyes, that smile, so beautiful… so captivating. It was the girl, the apparition from the night before!

My mind raced in bewilderment. My pulse quickened and I sat there mesmerized, unable to move, in complete and utter chaos of thought, at a loss for the presence of mind to grasp exactly what was going on.

Suddenly, the thunder crashed loudly in my ears and, less than a second later, the entire hangar lit up with a brilliant, blinding flash of light. I heard a loud crack from above as a beam from the roof truss let loose and I ducked down into the cockpit. The next thing I felt was a jolt to the back of my head, and in an instant my world went black. I drifted in and out of consciousness for a bit before finally having succumbed to the darkness.

Chapter 3

CLEAR! was the first word I heard as I started to come to. While it was ringing in my ears, I was reminded of countless emergency room scenes on television. In that instance, I thought I had died and I waited to feel the bone-jarring jolt of the defibrillator, hoping it would bring me back to life. I opened my eyes quickly, then I blinked at the blazing sun rising in the crisp, clear sky. It wasn't the voice of a doctor about to discharge 200 joules of life-saving electricity into my lifeless body; no, that was not the case. The voice was that of an aviation mechanic yelling to clear the propeller area as he swung the prop and started the engine of the airplane I was sitting in. I felt a firm slap on my right shoulder and heard a voice ask me if I was awake in there, meaning in the cockpit of the Eaglerock.

What had happened? It was only a moment before that I was lost and alone in a cool, dark hangar, sitting in the remnants of this old and rotting relic, and suddenly, I'd found myself dressed like a barnstormer, engine running, sunlight shimmering off the taut, fabric wings. I was lost and confused. I had no clue as to how I'd gotten there or how I would ever get back. I desperately wanted to make sense of it, but nothing made sense—nothing at all.

I looked around to try to establish where I was and to understand what was going on. To my left was a perfectly-groomed grass airstrip with a bright-orange windsock in the center of a lush emerald field. The sky was blue and clear with not a rain cloud in sight. The wind was calm. I looked to my right; the banner read, "1927 Winchester Fair." Further to the right still, a sign made of wood and cloth, "Fly 3 Dollars Fly!" Next to the sign, a line of people were waiting for their chance to leave the ground. I always loved that romantic period of aviation when seeing an airplane fly was not an everyday occurrence. Back then, now, or whenever it was, to go for an airplane ride was like getting a chance to fly in a space shuttle.

While I was looking around, my mechanic friend escorted my passenger to the front cockpit. With another slap on the shoulder, he brought me back to reality, if you could call it that. His voice raised above the rumble of the idling engine, he said, "She's all strapped in."

He looked at me for a long minute, dumbfounded as to why I hadn't yet started to taxi. When I realized what he was thinking, I did what any good pilot would do. I tossed aside the craziness of the situation, grabbed the stick, added a little burst of throttle, then I taxied away to take the young lady for her three-dollar airplane ride.

It seemed very natural at the time—insane, out of my mind, with no link to reality—but somehow natural. With another burst of throttle, I pressed on the rudder pedal and swung the little airplane around into the wind to start my takeoff roll. I eased forward on the stick ever so gently, let her accelerate a bit, then I lifted off into the sky with a gentle touch of back pressure on the control stick.

The woman in the front cockpit yelled just the slightest bit in a moment of joy as the earth fell away beneath the wheels, then she caught herself in an effort to remain ladylike in the midst of an adventure. I had never flown an Eaglerock before; I'd never even seen one outside of the walls of a museum, but I flew it that day as though I had been flying Eaglerocks for years. We climbed slowly into the sky and I followed as she pointed her way across the little town, over the church steeple in the square, and out past the lake to a small, white farmhouse with a charcoal roof. There was an older woman on the back porch whose arms flailed desperately in an attempt to get the young lady's attention. I circled for a bit. She waved wildly back, across the few hundred feet of summer sky, and she made a memory that will no-doubt endure the test of time for them both. I rocked the wings gently, a greeting of my own, then headed back toward the airfield.

I was enjoying the moment, watching her strawberry blonde hair floating in the breeze. Her perfume filled my senses and I was in a bit of a daze. I sat back and enjoyed the view: the lake, the town square, the church, the old cars, the blue sky, the young lady in front, then the crowd, and finally, the airstrip. With our little joyride coming to an end, I eased the Eaglerock into a sideslip while pulling the power to idle. My ears delighted in the sound of the soft whistle of the wind as it passed over the flying wires. I relaxed the controls out of the slip and settled the wheels to the grass in a gentle kiss of the earth, then added just a little power and taxied back to where we had started, cutting the engine in front of the crowd.

The mechanic returned and escorted the young lady from her seat. Before she stepped off the wing, she turned toward me. I was bewildered, blown away; my passenger was none other than the girl from the photograph. There she was, in living color, alive and well, stepping from the airplane. She leaned in and kissed my cheek and I swear it was electric, as if some sort of energy passed between us at that instant. She smiled and hurried over to her friends. Windblown and excited, she described her adventure aloft as they walked away giggling and laughing and I sat dumbfounded, unable to move. Then, she looked back once more and my heart raced at the sight of her beautiful blue eyes and that brilliant smile. I smiled back and in an instant she was gone, fading into the crowd.

"You ready to go again?" the mechanic yelled as loudly as if my engine was still running.

"Yeah," I replied, and he seated my next guest. He swung my prop once more and sent me on my way. I flew straight through for the next hour, then I stopped for fuel and something to eat after about my seventh passenger.

I looked for her every time we flew over the fair. I spotted her once by the cotton candy, but that was it.

So much had happened, so many out-of-this-world experiences, that my mind clung to the only thing I knew, the only thing that felt right—the flying. So I flew until sunset, passenger after passenger. Anthony, as I had come to know my mechanic's name, strapped the passengers in, collected the money and patted me on the shoulder, sending me on my way again and again until the sun began to fade and the evening came to a close.

Anthony and I topped off the fuel tank and wiped down the airplane to clean up the bugs and oil that had accumulated on it from the day's flying. We eased the Eaglerock into the hangar and pulled the covers over the cockpits, putting her to bed for the night. Anthony then pulled out a huge wad of cash, let out a joyful yell. "We really did good, kid," he said, "must be $150 here!"

A hundred-fifty dollars in 1927 money was quite a day's pay.

Chapter 4

My new-old friend and I walked together from the airfield. We strolled slowly down the foot path toward Main Street. The evening air glowed in silver moonlight, twinkling with diamond stars. It was breathtaking purity—calm, quiet, peaceful purity on that wooded path that evening. My day had left my mind scrambled; I didn't know for sure if I was in a dream or some altered state of reality. Thoughts were racing in and out of my mind, but that wooded path on the outskirts of that small Virginia town brought me an unexpected sense of inner peace. I looked at Anthony, detecting his smile through the darkness as he whistled softly in the night. He was at ease as well, and neither he nor I spoke until our path opened up at the edge of Main Street and the streetlights guided us down the cobblestone walk to the front door of his home.

Mary greeted us at the door. Tony's wife was a remarkably beautiful young woman with dark, friendly eyes and jet-black hair that flowed gracefully toward the center of her back. He kissed her softly and touched her hand, telling her with a smile of our earnings for the day. Then she opened the door to her home and greeted me with a gentle hug and kiss upon my cheek, the kind of greeting one reserves for family and those few friends that are considered as such.

We sat together and spoke well into the night as the conversation illuminated both my life and theirs. In what I could only describe as a parallel universe to my own, I evidently lived in a small apartment in their attic on the third floor of this meticulously well-kept home. Tony and I were friends ever since we'd spent time together during The Great War, he as a mechanic and myself as a pilot. After the war, we returned home together. We started barnstorming from town to town throughout Virginia, Pennsylvania, Ohio, Indiana and Illinois. After the three years that we had spent mostly on the road, Mary had pretty much had enough. She and Tony decided to settle down in Winchester and raise their family in some resemblance of a stable environment.

I, on the other hand, continued hopping from one small town to the next, living the only life I had come to know: fly over a town, pick a good field, do a bit of low-altitude acrobatics to pique the people's interest, and then spend my days selling rides to passengers and my nights sleeping beneath my wing. It was a free and wild existence, quite lucrative as well, but it was often lonely. My answer to the loneliness was my little apartment in the attic of my good friend's home. It was the only home I had. Every month or so, I would return there to regroup and touch base with my friend and his lovely family. Throughout the night, I had not once asked a direct question but rather gleaned this information over hours of dinner and card games interrupted only by Mary serving coffee and dessert and occasionally checking in on the children. Apparently, that day I had returned to Winchester to work with Anthony to sell rides at the county fair. Evidently, we never missed the fair. It was always profitable for both of us, and this year, the stream of riders seemed endless, as did the flow of cash that would help us make it through the winter.

With the pie and coffee gone, the conversation drifted from airplanes to children and the difficulties of supporting a family the size of the Anthony's. My friend decided it was time that I knew what he had been doing on the side to make additional money.

I was startled at first. I mean, running moonshine during Prohibition was illegal. Anthony took me to a small second bathroom they had installed at the end of a long hallway on the second floor of his home. It was complete with towels, washcloths, soap—all of the usual amenities. What struck me as strange was that it was all brand new, never used. The room sparkled and shined with remarkable cleanliness. Mary had been upstairs, evidently working in this room before our arrival. She turned to Tony and informed him that this batch was ready to be bottled.

He looked at me and smiled. "Bathtub gin," he said. "We make it, bottle it and I drive it to Norfolk along with some White Lightning from our still in the hidden basement of the barn. I always make my deliveries in the middle of the night to a contact who runs a speakeasy that caters to the needs of our servicemen. I make a good little profit and no one is the wiser."

I looked at the tub. It was half filled with a clear liquid. Tony grabbed a bottle after washing his hands and submersed it, letting it fill, then he removed it and sealed it with a cork. "One down," he said.
Seconds later, the whole house rattled with the pounding on the front door, and the hallways resounded with the calling of his name.

"Anthony Frane, Anthony Frane," the voice said, "this is Lieutenant Davidson. Open the door."

Tony ran to the stairs. I followed him as fast as I could. My legs were scrambling toward the front door in long, sprinting strides while my heart pounded so hard that I heard it racing inside my ears. Anxiety, adrenaline and a burst of exertion had me panting when I got to the foyer. The look on Tony's face was sheer terror; he really wasn't cut out for this kind of adventure. I couldn't believe what he had gotten us into. We were all going to be arrested if they found that bathtub full of gin.

The front door burst open. In a matter of seconds, the house was filled with revenuers. They started yelling at Tony, questioning the location of the alcohol. They pinned me against the wall, cuffed me, then sat me in a chair before starting an abrupt interrogation. I heard Mary scream from upstairs, then a door slammed so quickly that it echoed throughout the house. Moments later, a red-faced young man stumbled down the last steps, reporting to his superior,

"Nothing up there but a woman taking a bath."

He looked sheepishly toward Anthony and myself with an apology in his eyes and was still red in the face. In 20 minutes, they had gone through the entire house and found nothing. Tony had evidently become very good at keeping his secrets secret.

Later that evening, as we gathered once more at the kitchen table, Mary told us how she'd heard the agents screaming and not knowing what to do, she simply closed the door, slid the bottles into the closet and undressed, slipping into the clear gin as if she had just run a bath. When the agent opened the door, she screamed in embarrassment. He slammed the door shut, mumbling his apology, and proceeded, befuddled, stumbling back to the first floor to give his superior a rather awkward all-clear. That was pretty quick thinking, if you asked me. Mary had come up with a solution that no-doubt kept us all from some serious questioning and possible jail time, and it left me with a humorous story for years to come. We laughed and joked till the wee hours, then we headed off to our respective bedrooms. I fell asleep that night chuckling softly to myself as my eyes closed and the world went dark and silent around me.

Chapter 5

I awoke slowly, easing into the day was a boyhood habit which had carried through to my adult years. It always seemed as though my realization of my previous life was most evident in the first few waking moments of each day. That day, my first full day in 1927, I groggily stretched my arms then sat up on the edge of the bed. I was at first expecting to be back in my old home, in my own time, the whole experience nothing more than a dream.

That wasn't the case. Looking around, I quickly established myself to be exactly where I was when I drifted off to sleep after a rather adventurous day, in the early part of August, in the year of our Lord nineteen hundred and twenty-seven. The lace curtain drifted back and forth in the cool morning breeze. It brushed against my face, catching momentarily on my facial stubble as my head poked through to look out over the porch roof to the yard below. Tony was in the yard playing catch with Joey, his oldest son. I could hear them as they spoke. Tony was so kind, so involved in the young man's day-to-day life. You couldn't help but see the love that man carried for his children. I slid back against the headboard and closed my eyes, listening to the rhythmic slap of the ball against the glove and the laughter of the young man as his father joked with him about his newfound interest in the girls from the lake. It was a pleasant way to start a summer morning. In my relaxed state, my mind wandered. What exactly was it that had happened to me? How did I get to this place, this time?

My mind was coming in and out of a state of disbelief. In 24 hours, I had somehow managed to escape airplane-shattering thunderstorms, discover a hauntingly-beautiful photograph in a relic of an old airplane, travel through time to find my consciousness in 1927, get the first kiss from my soulmate and find myself in the middle of a raid on the moonshining operation of my new-old friend Tony. I wasn't sure if I was dreaming or not. All I can tell you is that the opportunity to return to my previous life never materialized. I never had a time machine or an identifiable portal. One minute, I was sitting in a relic in an old hangar when a sudden crash of thunder and flash of lightning brought an old support beam crashing down upon me. The next thing I knew, I was a barnstormer completely engulfed in all that was going on around me. If the moment to return came, and it was my choice, I probably would never return. There were people that needed me here and, more importantly, there was the ever-present lore of the most beautiful woman I had ever seen who electrified my existence.

Those thoughts ran through my mind and I started to mentally liken my situation to that of a European immigrant at the turn of the century. Those brave souls left behind every bit of the world they knew in quest of an entirely new existence in the United States, or the New World as it was called. In my case, it was more of a new universe.

Many years later, I confided in a friend and neighbor who made his living as a quantum physicist about the whole time travel thing. He did not try to have me committed, but instead, went off into the layman's explanation of the "many worlds" interpretation of quantum physics—the fact that at any given time there are many universes running parallel to one another. Some scientists believe that each person has a presence in the multiple universes and that may or may not be on the same timeline. He went on to tell me that my consciousness might have shifted from one parallel universe to another, hence the timeline shift and other inexplicable events. It was all very confusing, even though he presented it the best he could at a level that I might grasp. The parallel universe theory is not the story here, though. It's just a vessel that changed my world and let me attempt to understand what had happened to me. My story goes on from that moment in the bed with my head resting against the headboard. In that initial stream of thought, as the morning breeze blew gently across my face, and my friend and his son laughed and joked in the sunshine, I found a certain peace with my situation. I decided to commit myself to the life I had in front of me, help my friends, Tony and Mary, and, most importantly, find the girl, the apparition who started this quest.

My eyes still closed, I heard a car idle to a stop in front of the house. The rhythmic slap of their game of catch ceased almost immediately and I heard Tony's tone change to one of fatherly sternness as he sent Joey into the house. My eyes

popped open as I heard Tony arguing with a man in the front yard. The well-dressed man looked like something out of a gangster movie complete with his two goons, one on each side. He wore a pinstriped suit with a dress hat. His shoes were polished so brightly that they reflected the sun. He was pointing at Tony. His threatening demeanor emanated through the morning silence and my open window.
I ran down the stairs to see what was going on. Just as I opened the door, the man to the right of Tony took a swing at him. It was a cheap shot, really, right in the middle of the suit's speech, while Tony was distracted. Tony fell to his knees in pain and struggled to get himself back up. He had the wind knocked out of him and was gasping for air as the man to his left pulled his leg back to kick Tony while he was down. I ran and dove from the porch, tackling the kicker as my momentum carried us through the rose bushes to the busted-up sidewalk that ran next to the street.

I came out on top and started swinging. I still can't remember the blow-by-blow of the altercation. The next thing I recall is one man out cold beneath me with blood on his face and blood dripping from my right hand.

Mary was screaming from the porch. "Stop, stop!" she cried. I looked back toward the yard and Tony was on top of the other goon, choking him, and now he was the one gasping for air. Just then, the suit ran to his car and emerged with a pistol from the glove box. Our hands went into the air immediately as we tried to avoid getting shot while the suit took control of the situation.

The suit looked to the man who was crawling to his feet over by Tony and instructed him to help his cohort into the car with a disappointed look and a wave of the pistol. The pistol slid into his vest just as an officer pulled up beside his car. The suit approached the police car and had a little discussion with the officer behind the wheel, shaking his hand and nodding in agreement with the officers warnings. I'm not certain how much he slipped the sergeant during that little handshake, but the officer sure seemed to become more friendly toward the gangster as the suit stepped away claiming it was all a big misunderstanding.

Then, he looked to Tony and in his deep movie gangster voice, he said, "Just remember what I told you."

He turned back toward his car, took the driver's seat and drove away. The two young police officers spoke with Tony briefly, and he explained away the bloodied hand and limping gangsters to some sort of misunderstanding, unintentionally corroborating the gangsters' story. He claimed the suited gentleman was just a little overzealous and had the wrong guy and that we were just defending ourselves. The police officers nodded their heads and pulled away. No one was pressing any charges that day. Like two warriors fresh from the battlefield, Tony and I limped arm in arm up the stairs and across the battered, wooden porch. We ambled to the front door that Mary held open for us. I waited a few minutes in silence as we sat at the kitchen table and Mary poured us each a cup of coffee.

Tony seemed almost embarrassed as he started to speak. He explained to me that my rude awakening was due to the fact that the little moonshine operation he had started had become a little too successful and had begun to cut into the profit margins of the suit and his buddies. They ran a well-organized, well-funded still that pretty much dominated the area. Tony, trying his hand at a little economic subsidy and succeeding, was not going to be tolerated.

I didn't have to be a genius to realize Tony had no place with these guys. They were there to inform my friend that, according to their calculations, he owed the suit $10,000 for his cut of the moonshine business Tony had stolen from him.

His voice trembled as he spoke that number. "Ten thousand dollars!" In all the time he had been selling moonshine, he had never even made this much money. The suit knew this, but his threat still stood. It was a general threat: "Bad things happen."

After a somewhat relaxing soak in the claw foot tub, I dried off and used some bandages from Mary's cabinet to cover the wounds on my right hand. Evidently, in my red-out I literally saw red and I really didn't remember much else. I must have beaten my opponent with one hand. The left hand was fine.

Clean and dry, I went back downstairs to talk with Tony. He was no longer in the kitchen. When I asked for him, Mary just smiled politely and pointed me to the backyard. She was a strong, silent woman of great beauty whose eyes showed such kindness even when she was angry. Mary lived for her children, and they were always the first thought in any situation. She had put her faith in Tony, although his recent endeavors brought with them such risk and such limited reward that she had been begging him from the very start to leave the moonshining business behind. Perhaps with the increased danger, Tony would see his way clear to step away from it all. That was her wish at the time. All I knew when she pointed me toward the backyard was that the glow had left her eyes. She was not just angry; she was fearful for the well-being of the ones she loved. It was a fear that she suppressed. She never showed the deep fear she held inside to the children. They had already been exposed to too much.

Chapter 6

In the backyard, Tony was strapping some fishing gear to two motorcycles. He looked up at me and smiled.

"We've got a few hours before we start flying today," he said. "I thought we could get a little fishing in, maybe give us a chance to talk?"

I smiled back. "Sure, I think we need to talk."

Then I hopped on the army-green Harley and jumped on the kick starter. Tony slapped me on the shoulder, looking surprised. Then he stared coldly. "I can start my own bike, thanks."

I hid my embarrassment and slinked over to the red and gold Indian, then jumped twice on the kick starter before it rumbled to life. As the bikes spit and coughed, the rough idles filled the air around us. Tony asked if I was feeling alright.

I paused and looked at him. "Just a little sore from the whole fight thing."

I had ridden motorcycles since I was a kid, but unlike the Eaglerock, this old motorcycle just wasn't coming to me. I stalled for time, rubbing my head with my hand as I watched Tony step on the clutch then shift the bike into first gear with a shift knob next to the gas tank similar to that of a lawn tractor. He revved the engine and eased out the clutch with his left foot as the bike leapt forward.

"Wanna race?" he yelled when he pulled way.

Having a great deal of experience riding, I adapted rather quickly, mimicking Tony's actions with one exception: I over-revved the engine and dumped the clutch to prevent the bike from stalling before I could get the hang of it. The result was a dust-generating, rock-spewing rear wheel as I raced off to catch him. Tony led and I kept adjusting my shifting technique as we sped off together down the old dirt road toward the lake. It was such a beautiful day. We were riding together on these fantastic old machines through the summer countryside, and it felt as though it were a dream. My technical difficulties soon faded and I began to ride like I had been riding these old bikes all my life. Perhaps, in this universe, I had.

Wildflowers spilled over from the fields, overshadowing the dry dirt road, and lush green trees filled the sky above us. Their shade cooled us as we bounced along, enjoying our high-speed stroll. I hung back from Tony to avoid his exhaust and to have the chance to breathe in deeply the oxygen-rich air and soak up the feel of the sun on my skin. I really started to enjoy my time in the tan, leather saddle of that old Indian, feeling free and exhilarated at the same time. Thinking back, I can see why motorcycles were always a part of my life.

When we got to the lake that day, my morning vistas continued. I always loved the look of sunlight reflected in the ripples of the water. That morning, the sun provided the lake with a silver-gold sheen as we looked out across it. We unpacked the rods and baited our hooks, then we cast almost simultaneously from the water's edge. After a few minutes of silence, Tony pulled in his first fish, a large-mouth bass that was itself quite large. He started to speak.

"I never wanted to let this whole moonshine thing get out of hand," he said emotionally. "It all started as a simple way to make a few extra dollars to help with the surgery on little Mike's foot. I just wish there was a way out. I can't come up with the money they are demanding so I'll keep selling moonshine to try and pay them off and protect my family.

"Meanwhile, he keeps raising the price tag. It's a catch-22 where I do all the work and he makes all the money. I haven't made any progress in saving towards the surgery. That was the reason I got involved with this whole mess to begin with. I don't know which way to turn on this one, my friend."

Tony's bobber sank beneath the surface; another sizable catch. I understood his motivation and even admired his resourcefulness, but between the law and the gangsters, I could see that he had certainly chosen the wrong direction. I explained my concern for him and his family and vowed to help them in any way I could if he promised to leave the moonshining business. He went on.

"You understand, don't you? I really don't have a choice anymore. I can't let that guy take advantage of me," he said desperately. "I have to find a way to beat him at his own game."

I just raised an eyebrow and nodded a soft 'yes,' though I really wished he were smarter and less prideful. During our conversation, Tony had been pulling in the fish left and right. He baited again and in two minutes had yet another tug on the line. As he reeled it in he looked my way and smiled.

"Not biting today?" Tony chuckled. "Hang in there, buddy. I'm headed back to the house."

Then he hopped on his bike with his pannier filled with his catch. It started with just one kick and he smiled over his shoulder.

"We'll work this out," he said, "we always do."

"I'm staying until I catch something—anything," I replied.

He laughed and roared away. I turned back toward the lake and my fishing rod. I sat there alone with plenty of time to think. My friend was a loving, kind and generous man, a man whose existence depended on the love of his wonderful family. He was caught in a bad situation that made an honorable man struggle with the fringes of illegal activity. As a result, he was being sucked further and further into the darkness. I couldn't let that happen. I had to help him. If I could just get that gangster to back off, maybe then I could find a way, a legal way, to help Tony get the money he needed for his son.

I knew these things rarely worked out well when the mob was involved, but I had to try. I decided to go and have a talk with the suit to see if we could come to some sort of an agreement. At that time, I didn't even know his name, but I felt as though finding him would not be all that difficult. His type seemed to always show up whether they were welcome or not.

Fishing became my priority of the moment. I sat on a large rock beneath an old oak tree at the water's edge with my fishing rod in hand. The sunlight pierced through the branches and I leaned back into the beam of warmth. My eyes eased shut. I was calm and peaceful, waiting for a tug on the line. The gentle lapping of the water on the rocks put me into a trance-like state and I settled in. It was not your standard approach to fishing, but it was a peacefulness that I just could not resist after all that I had been through in recent days. Birds chirping, the water lapping against the shore, the warmth of the sun: it was a peaceful summer day.

It seemed just the slightest bit strange at first. The rhythm of the water against the shore faded and I began to hear a sloshing noise in the distance coming from the lake. It held its own rhythm and grew closer and closer to me with every second. I opened my eyes and squinted into the sun-drenched lake, trying to identify the source of the odd noise.

I caught sight of her just as the sloshing ceased and she pulled herself from the water onto the large rock to my left. She stood atop that rock, not 30 feet from me. Then, in one graceful motion, she removed her bathing cap and let her strawberry-blonde hair flow freely over her shoulders. With the sun behind her and the water glistening on her skin, her appearance was angelic. I was taken completely by surprise.

I could hear my heartbeat pounding in my ears as I tried to summon the courage to speak to her. She had such an effect on every cell of my body. It was the most rare, most unique feeling I had ever felt and all she had done was come into my sight.

She was real—the girl from the apparition, the cockpit photo, my passenger. She was real and sitting before me on the rocks with her head tilted back and her long hair flowing gracefully behind her as she let the sun dry her from her swim. In the past, I had argued against the idea of a soulmate, one person made for another, destined to be together. Those moments on the shore I knew that she was my soulmate, that she would be my wife. I calmly leaned up against the tree, then I rose to my feet and headed toward the motorcycle.

I didn't want to startle her; rather, I thought I would make it look as if she had discovered me. She, of course, did not discover me. Thirty feet away sat the girl of my dreams basking in the morning sun, completely immersed in her thoughts and oblivious to my existence. (Years later she would confess that she knew I was there and was feeling the same biochemical attraction, but had chosen to stay put and allow me to stumble about, trying to figure a way to say hello.)

I pulled an old towel from the pannier on the back of the bike. It was covered in grease. I stuffed it back inside. That wouldn't do. I searched for something to help me break the ice and nervously reached into my pocket to find a pack of gum, Beeman's Gum. It was the gum of the aviator I'd seen in so many movies in years before, and there it was in my hand. I walked carefully over and leaned against the tree as I unwrapped a stick of gum and started to chew. The closer I got, the more beautiful she was.

"Hi," I said. Not the smoothest opening, but it would do. She opened her eyes and looked in the direction of my voice. Her sweet, blue eyes met my gaze and the strangest thing happened. She said “hello,” and all of the tension melted away. For some reason, I was never again nervous to talk with her. Over the years, our conversations always flowed. From that very moment, something started between us. The conversations came so easily. It was effortless. We exchanged names, and I liked the way hers sounded as it came from her lips: "Maura."

She teased me about being the fly boy from the county fair. I teased her back about kissing my cheek as she left my airplane.

"Oh, you remember that?" she said.

Coy again, but not entirely truthful, as she later admitted to being overwhelmed, the kiss following her attraction before she could stop herself. We spoke for nearly an hour, sitting next to one another on the rocks by the lake. The topics ranged from high school to puppy dogs to our chosen professions.

She worked as a nurse in the local hospital. I remember thinking it was a noble profession that helped so many people every single day. She was witty and intelligent and her nose wrinkled just a little bit when she laughed. When God was passing out charm, that young lady had received a double dose. I abandoned my fishing rod and strolled along the shore path, trying to learn all that I could about this mesmerizing young lady. When we returned to the rock she had appeared on, we talked and laughed some more. I never wanted the morning to end, but of course it had to, and it did so in a rather alarming way.

A raucous noise drew my attention to the road and I rose to my feet to see who was coming. A sleek maroon and tan Packard sped along the dirt road in the distance. She started to stand and I offered her a hand up. Her eyes met mine as our hands first touched and I felt it again, that chemistry between us, so strong she could hardly hide it behind her baby blues. She stood and I noticed her figure, her beautiful, graceful, athletic body with just the right amount of soft curves. Everything about the woman was perfect. I looked away politely as she caught my glance.

My heart started pounding again as the car drew near. I couldn't believe it! I knew that car. It was the suit! He was probably coming to tend to me once and for all after our altercation earlier that morning. It wasn't looking good for me. He seemed like the type of guy that rarely traveled alone. I would be outnumbered and beaten and, at the very least, embarrassed in front of the girl of my dreams. She looked at the car, then she looked at me, staring at it as he skidded to a stop.

She smiled. "Do you know Ray?" I smirked in response as she grabbed her cap. "I have to go," she said. "My friends are here to pick me up."

She greeted the suit and another couple, then she slipped into the passenger seat. Ray leaned in as if to give her a kiss. She pushed him away and slid toward the door then waved politely as they sped off. I coughed on the rising dust, then I turned and walked toward the shore, shaking my head in disbelief. To top it all off, I watched as my only bite of the day pulled on my bamboo rod and swam away with it.

Chapter 7

I spent the rest of the morning enjoying the country roads on the rumbling old Indian, then I returned to have lunch with Tony and Mary. After lunch, Tony and I walked to the fairgrounds and I told him of my encounter with the bathing beauty. He laughed and put his hand on my shoulder, and in a cautious tone, he warned me of her friend. He said if the suit, Ray being his real name, ever got wind of me talking to his girl, it could get pretty ugly pretty quickly and that we both needed to find a way to separate ourselves from his far-reaching influence.

We spent that afternoon selling biplane rides again at the fair. It was amazing to me just how many people would come out and spend their hard-earned money for a taste of the freedom of flight. It was a different era back then when an airplane ride was a rare occurrence. It was not the flight of the airlines, it was pure flight—out in the open air, with the wind pouring over you as you flew low and slow over the town you grew up in. Spending those minutes in the air had a profound effect on the people we flew; it changed them. Their minutes aloft brought real adventure into their lives. I was honored to be a part of that adventure and to make them feel courageous and without limits as they roared through the sky in my old biplane.

Every time we took a break, I wandered the fairgrounds looking for Maura. I wanted so badly to see her, to speak with her again. The threat of Ray would not stop me. It wasn't much of a choice; I had to see her again—she dominated my every thought. Three times that day, the last day of the fair, I wandered aimlessly in search of her, and all three times I came up empty. I thought perhaps her feelings were not the same as mine and that she was not putting forth any effort to contact me again. My mood dampened further with each unsuccessful search. Perhaps it was just too good to be true, I thought.

I didn't notice it at first as I crawled back into the cockpit for the final flight of the evening. The sun was fading toward the horizon and the western sky glowed in varied shades of red, gold, and magenta. Studying the sky, I knew the day had but one flight left in it and that it would be the most visually spectacular flight of the day. I gave my sales pitch three times and only one man stepped forward.

"Make it a good one," he yelled as he leaned back when Tony was strapping him in.

As I taxied out onto the grass strip, I looked at the cockpit panel in front of me. There, in the lower right corner of the Eaglerock's instrument panel, was Maura's picture wedged against the molding. I smiled to myself and pushed the throttle toward the firewall. In seconds, we were airborne and I showed my exuberance for the moment in the flight. I'm sure my passenger told tales of that flight for many years to come. We climbed toward the sky, grabbing for altitude, then leveled off and accelerated into a series of barrel rolls, wing over wing over wing. I dove toward the ground with the wind singing in the flying wires, then I pulled back smoothly on the stick.

My passenger screamed as he stared out over the engine, cowling, and I exchanged Earth for sky and then back to Earth again. Out of the bottom of the loop we shot, speeding, 100 feet above the ground into another loop, then rolled the little airplane over into an Immelmann. I cut the power and the plane fell quiet, save the sound of the wind as the propeller turned softly at idle, and I glided the Eaglerock to safety on the grass.

I was smiling from ear to ear in a celebration of the fact that Maura must have cared for me as well. The picture with her address on the back was her show of affection. With that perfect gesture, my world lit up and I had launched into the sky, enjoying the twisting and turning of my world. I flew, watching the emerald fields and the amber glowing of the setting sun, in the promise of the excitement that loomed. My rider just shook my hand as he wobbled from the plane, a little weak in the knees, and I slipped the three dollars back to him. I'm not sure he was sharing in my enthusiasm.

Chapter 8

It was dark when Tony and I put on the cockpit covers and rolled the Eaglerock back into our makeshift hanger. He took our earnings from the day and stuffed them into his backpack. We walked once more along the path toward town, each of us smiling to ourselves for different reasons.

It wasn't her long, flowing hair, or the curves of her body in the moonlight, that drew my attention. It was her smile that kept me staring a bit longer than I should have. That universal expression of warmth made her glow with kindness in the midst of the moonlit night. I introduced Tony briefly, then he nodded and said he was heading home and he would see me there. She extended her hand and I placed mine in hers as our second touch quickly became our first embrace, and I felt the softness of her lips in a moment I shall treasure forever.

There've been stories of love at first sight told throughout the world in books and movies. Until I met Maura, I never believed they could be true. Our hearts and minds were one, brought together in a synergy of the soul. Together, we were more alive than the sum of our energies apart. In years to come, that synergy would cause the ache in my chest and the longing I felt to return anytime that I was away from her.

The night fell upon the lake and the reflection of the moon caught the gentle ripples as a small rowboat glided past. We walked along the path to the rock ledge where we had spoken earlier that day. I sat and leaned against the tree. She sat between my legs, her head against my chest, looking out at the lake in the moonlight. We talked for hours. It was an exciting, open conversation that brought her past to life. Every story was a chapter of her life. Every chapter drew me closer to her. She even told me of Ray, the suit, and the brief time she spent dating him and of his unrequited love for her after the relationship ended.

She brought me right up to the point in time where we had met and told me of the stirrings of her heart on a sunny summer day in an awkward conversation with a motorcyclist-fly boy who consumed her thoughts from that moment forward. I shared my feelings as well, and I wrapped my arms around her as the last remaining clouds drifted away, revealing the dazzling, starlit sky. Just above the tree line, in the distance, a meteor streaked in front of us. It was a riveting blaze that sped away and faded out of our sight.

She seemed so comfortable and at ease with me, and I heard her sigh gently as her head eased back against my chest once more. The night sky was a thing of beauty; she was beautiful, and we had started into the relationship that would define my years on this planet. Our conversation eventually fell silent as we gazed at the stars, then, in just a few minutes, Maura drifted off. I spoke her name softly and realized she had fallen asleep in my arms. I sat in quiet appreciation, looking off into the night sky with the girl of my dreams curled up against me. I began to wonder if perhaps I was caught within a dream, trapped inside the confines of my mind.

Everything felt real to me: the tree behind my back, her head on my chest, yet, how could I have been transported to this time? It didn't make any sense. There was no logical path from home in the future to this time in what appeared to me to be a distant past. There I was, though, in one of the happiest moments of my life filled with a sense of calm, knowing that it was where I belonged. My travel had been through time rather than space, but like that immigrant I mentioned, I was so caught up in my new world, my new life, that the past/future held no relevance. I simply accepted my life as it had become. It dawned on me, as my thoughts ran deeper than the lake I looked out upon, that it was all about her. That I had to be there during that time to be with her. God had a plan and that plan required me to undergo a journey that utilized an adjustment in my own personal timeline. I had traveled to meet my soulmate, and my destiny knew no boundaries be they space or time. I realized that love was, in and of itself, timeless.

The lapping of the lake against the shore put me to sleep as well with her held in my arms. Minutes or hours later, I'm not sure, I woke to her gentle kiss upon my cheek in the soft glow of the moon and the starlit sky.

"I have to go, it's getting late," she whispered. I walked her to her house, then I kissed her once more beneath the weeping cherry tree in her front yard. She hurried quietly through the doorway and I strolled home. My thoughts were only of Maura and our evening at the lake.

Chapter 9

Over the next few months, I spent my weekdays working as a mechanic in Tony's garage. Tony and I fixed anything with a motor: cars, tractors, motorcycles—anything. It was great getting to really know Tony as we worked side by side. My friend lived for his children. He was always so proud of them; he truly doted over those kids, and they were the reason behind everything that the man did. He lived for his family and cherished his evenings with them. If it wasn't baseball with his boys, he was helping his daughters host tea parties. Love exuded from my tough-guy friend everytime one of his nine children came to mind.

Working in Tony's garage also gave me an opportunity to spend my evenings with Maura. We grew closer every day. Our relationship always had its own pace, a fast, adventurous pace. On the weekends, if the weather was good, Maura and I would head off in the biplane to nearby fairs, meeting up with Tony, who always drove to meet us with one of his children in tow. I taught her to fly the airplane and each trip offered a multitude of lessons aloft. By the end of two months, she was capable of taking off and landing by herself. At the fairs, Maura would sell the tickets; Tony would load and unload the passengers and keep the airplane in top shape; and I would barnstorm, taking the passengers where only birds and angels dared to go! We had a lot of fun on those weekends, making small fortunes as we traveled throughout the state together.

Every Sunday night when we returned, Maura and I would go to dinner at her mother's house. Maura lived with her mom, a strong, thin, lively woman with short, blonde hair and thin-rimmed glasses who absolutely cherished her daughter. She wanted to rule with a firm hand, but kindness was the example she set for her only child, the light of her life.

Maura followed her rules, for the most part, more out of respect than fear. The early death of her dad brought Maura and her mom even closer as they took care of each other over the years. Her father had passed away in the war. He was a Naval officer on a battleship who died heroically, trying to save another man's life as the ship they were manning sank. The U.S.S. San Diego sank off the coast of Nantucket due to a boiler explosion that is believed to have been secondary to the explosion of a German mine. The other man survived, making his way to a lifeboat, but Maura's father did not.

Our all consuming courtship was enhancing our feelings for one another. Every day was filled with thoughts of Maura and the endorphin rush that overflowed into every aspect of our lives. My life with her was pure joy. We felt so blessed with such a fulfillment and passion that the days and nights passed by in a blur. It was a whirlwind in a time of our lives where everything seemed to be going right for us.

Certain things I remember as clearly as the day they happened: it was October 8th, 1927. I awoke to the sunlight streaming through the curtains of my bedroom and looked out the window at the autumn leaves on the old oak tree in front of Tony and Mary's house. In short order, Maura's voice brought a smile to my face. I heard her downstairs. She was speaking and laughing with Mary. I showered quickly and ran to greet her. Maura was standing there in her hiking clothes, a five-foot-three, strawberry-blonde beauty dressed for an outdoor adventure. When my feet hit the final step I grabbed her, hugging her as I kissed her good morning. She had come by to offer me the chance to go hiking with her to a place called McAfee Knob, a beautiful day hike along what would eventually become the Appalachian Trail.

We rode the motorcycle to the trailhead along an old dirt road, bundled with layers of clothing to keep us warm. It was a multicolored blast across the countryside that in and of itself would have been enough enjoyment for one day. Then we hiked off into the woods for hours through the covered trails that kept us both shaded and refreshed. Finally, a short, steep switchback opened into a vast plain of rock and one of the most spectacular views I had ever seen with my feet still planted on terra firma. The long, thin rock jutted out dangerously over the valley for a good 30 feet. The view was filled with rolling hill after rolling hill, covered in splashes of red, orange, brown, yellow and green as far as the eye could see. A shimmering lake glistened in the morning sun off to the east, and a ribbon of a river flowed gently away, fading on the horizon.

We were alone, feeling as if we had the whole world to ourselves. Her kiss sent explosions of hormones racing through my body and I felt more for her in those moments than I had ever felt for any other person in my entire life. Many people feel such passion in the dawning of a new relationship, but for us, the feeling never went away. The love of my life, that glimmering star of a woman atop the autumn mountains of Virginia, remained with me every single day of our lives. At 85 years old, this very night, as I kissed her forehead just before she faded off to sleep and I started to write this memory, her inner light still glowed in an ongoing love affair that has never skipped a beat.

By the time we hiked the path to that mountaintop I knew that I was in love with her, and the way she looked so deeply into my eyes, I knew that she loved me too. The sun shined brightly in the azure sky, a majestic bald eagle was circling above our heads, and we shared our sandwich and canteen of water, overlooking the world in each other's arms from the terrace of nature's mansion. Our feet dangled freely over the edge.

After lunch, we climbed back to the safety of the rock ledge and I asked her to reach into the backpack for our compass. She found the small box with the red ribbon tied so neatly in a bow. There on the top of that mountain in our couples' solitude, I dropped to one knee and asked her to be my wife. She pulled the ribbon free and I placed the ring on her left hand. Her exuberance echoed through the valley and our return to the foot of the mountain was filled with excitement. I remember feeling like the luckiest man alive, unknowing in our joy that there would be many trials to face before our life together would be free of the overshadowing presence that just refused to leave us be.

In our moments of happiness I didn't think much about it, but as we were descending the mountain, there was a man that I knew I had seen before who climbed past us. He offered no greeting; he stopped at the top of the path and pulled out a cigarette, then he stood there smoking as he kept following us with his gaze until we walked out of his sight. Looking back on it, I am sure he was one of Ray Vitale's men. In fact, when I scanned my memory, there always seemed to be someone lurking about, even when we thought we were off on our own. Whether passing rowboats or strange solo hikers with no hiking gear, someone was always around us.

When we got back to the house, Tony and two of his children, Emma and Charlotte, were playing in the yard. The children's voices rang with laughter as their Dad chased them in a playful game of monkey in the middle. Tony was, of course, the monkey. I went inside to put away our packs and Maura stayed behind. When I came back out, Maura and Mary were in a conversation about the joys of motherhood as Mary watched her husband banter back and forth, teasing his two youngest girls.

Tony was such a friend to me and a perfect example of a loving husband and doting father. Looking on from the porch, I couldn't help but notice how great a Dad he was and my thoughts flashed to the hopes that someday I, too, would share in the blessings of my own family. We shared the news of our engagement with our friends and they insisted on taking us out to celebrate. It was a joyous night on the town with Maura and me as the honored guests.

Chapter 10

After dinner, Tony and I headed back to the airport together to start to prepare the airplane for winter storage. Now that all the fairs had ended, we would take the appropriate measures to store the airplane and make it easier to ready it in the spring for another season of barnstorming. It was time-consuming and, by the time the Eaglerock was rolled to the back of the hangar, night had fallen. We walked together from the airport to Tony's house, laughing and joking in the moonlight. He was unrelenting as he ribbed his old friend who had fallen hard for the petite little redhead from across the lake. I blushed in embarrassment, but he never knew, as the darkness had come to my rescue. It had been an eventful and productive year for our little barnstorming business and for our relationships as well.

Halfway down the path, the horizon lit up. Raging red filled the sky with blazing shards of orange and yellow that rose into the night. We raced to its source, fearing for the worst. Then, we realized our fears had become reality.

Mary stood by the fire truck, screaming the name of her youngest daughter as the blaze consumed the barn. Emma was nowhere to be found. Tony and I raced together toward the fire as the fireman's hose made futile attempts to douse the flames. Just as we entered the barn, an explosion within blew us back to the street. Tony and I were knocked momentarily unconscious. We awoke to the horror of the flames and staggered slowly to our feet.

Tony screamed his daughter's name into the night, but it was of no use, for as the morning light broke and the fire finally quelled, Emma's lifeless body lay in the stall where she sought refuge. She had died from the smoke, surrounded by terrifying flames. At her side was the beloved dog that she attempted to rescue when the fire broke out.

My heart crumbled in an instant, a little piece of me dying along with Emma.

Earlier that night, on the walk home, Tony had smiled his last smile, for as little Emma had taken with her a piece of my heart, she had also taken all that was my best friend. Tony never recovered; his daughter had lost her life, and my friend had lost his way.

For the months that followed, Tony found his peace in the very same thing that had caused the death of Emma. He was lost in a drunken stupor day in and day out. Over time, we found out that the bonfire was set intentionally. Ray Vitale—the suit, as I referred to him—was well-connected to the wrong type of people, the type of people who would burn down the still in order to erase Ray's competition. They set fire to Tony's barn that night to teach Tony a lesson, and that lesson was hard-learned. Now, Tony was consumed in the grief of his loss. He calmed his mind with the same exact substance that caused his problems to begin with. I spent hours, then days and eventually months, trying to help my friend to move beyond the grief. I was caught in the frustration of enabling or ignoring his suffering. Loss is hard to deal with, and Tony not only felt loss—he felt guilt.

Over the next few months, Maura and I helped Mary with Tony and the kids. We did what we could to guide and strengthen our extended family. Mary would weep in silence after the children were put to bed, but in the mornings, she would be the strong and guiding force that shaped their lives. My relationship with Maura grew with each passing day, and the harsh events strengthened us rather than tore us apart. Maura was a strong woman as well, much like Mary. Seeing her in crisis made me appreciate the inner strength of the beautiful woman that would soon share my life.

As strong as Maura was, she was hiding something from me. She feared the wrath of Raymond Vitale. One night, she had bumped into Ray at the hospital. She tried to ignore him, but he followed her. Cornering her in an empty hallway, he begged for her forgiveness. He pleaded for a chance to restore their friendship and keep open, at least in his mind, the opportunity for a romantic relationship.

She wanted nothing to do with him. After seeing what he had done, she despised the man and wanted to stay as far away from him as possible. Maura thwarted his advances and shut him down cold. His eyes filled with rage. She watched in terror as the fury boiled over inside him. He lunged at her and grabbed her by the throat, cursing her out, calling her every name in the book. Then he told her that he had already dug two graves in the woods, one for her and one for me.

"It may not be today or tomorrow or next month or even next year, but when you least expect it, I will come for you both, and your bodies will never be found," was his direct quote to her.

Then he tossed her to the ground and huffed away. What he said was a scary thought that put her on guard at all times, yet she kept it from me for months, fearing that I would confront him and be murdered in the process. It was becoming harder and harder for her to keep that confrontation a secret, as either Ray or his goons were always about in the small town. Ray was growing more and more angry with the fact that Maura had left him behind.

She finally shared her concerns and a portion of the story with me, leaving out the assault, but allowing me knowledge of the threats he had made. As her story came to light, she revealed that she'd dated Ray briefly a few years prior and that he relentlessly tried to get her back, always threatening to hurt anyone that she would even consider dating. He seared with envy at the site of us together and that was growing more and more evident.

I promised Maura that I would keep my cool. On the other hand, I secretly longed for a chance to confront Ray. At the time, my deep-seated anger toward him continued to grow as the truth of that barn fire came to light. I felt Ray Vitale was responsible for Emma's death and for all of the suffering that Tony and Mary had known. Now he wanted us to live our lives in fear. This could not go unchecked. I would have to do something.

Chapter 11

It was a Tuesday night in January of 1928 when Maura and I huddled into a corner booth at Vicky's Restaurant on Fifth Street. Tony stumbled in. He was drunk. His jacket was half off his shoulder and his nose was busted from a fall he must've taken; he was a mess. He slurred a 'hello' in our direction and I called him over to our table, then I ordered him a coffee and handed him a menu.

I tried again to reach him, to find my friend inside the shell of a man that he had become. Reasoning would not work, I knew that, but I had to try—I just had to. Looking at my friend in that booth, I could not find a single remnant of the man whose medal of honor hung on the wall in his den. Tony, to all appearances, was gone. My heart ached once more, but I smiled and did all that I could do. I sat with Tony, entertaining the slurred remembrances of the life he led. It was uncomfortable for me, and for Maura as well, but we listened in earnest to his past as we pitied his present state.

Tony rose from the table and staggered off toward the restroom. Maura pulled out a picture from her purse. She had been looking at a house earlier that day, and she had a picture of it to show me. It was a beautiful little Cape Cod house, bluish-grey with red shutters and a white picket fence. Three small dormers jutted out from the second floor. We were hoping to buy something small that we could fix up together as our first home after we got married.

Studying the details of the photograph, we were lost in the thought of a brighter future for a few moments—so lost in those thoughts that we never even heard the bell jingle as the front door opened and then closed again. I looked up toward the restroom to see Tony heading in our direction, when suddenly, my view was blocked by two very large men in pinstripe suits. I raised my head to ask what they wanted as they stood just four feet in front of me. The one on the left blocked our exit from the booth and the one on the right spoke out in a gravelly voice.

"Ray Vitale says if you want her, you can have her," he mumbled.

Then he reached into his pocket and pulled out a vile. He immediately uncapped it and tossed the contents directly at Maura's face. The acid made a steady stream through the air as the other big goon pinned me against the booth. But somehow, when he was needed the most, Tony had come to life. The hero within him rose to the occasion and he launched his body between Maura and the assailant.

The acid immediately made the skin on Tony's face boil and peel, big welts emerging from his chest as he lay gasping for air. The two henchmen dashed for the door and we hurried to Tony's side. With a wet towel compressed against his skin, we rushed Tony to the doctor across the street.

Tony died later that night from complications of the acid attack. His lungs had been burned to the point that he could no longer breathe. The funeral service honored Tony as a war hero; we knew him as the hero who had saved Maura's life. He died so that she could live. My friend came through when I'd least expected his act of pure bravery in order to save the love of my life.

I wept that night in Maura's arms, then I gathered myself and wiped the tears from her eyes as I held her tightly. We drew our strength from each other, for we both had lost a good friend. Those last months since the death of his daughter were not his best, but his final action proved that, beneath the grief and sorrow, the man that he truly was had lived on. He was a hero at heart, and that is how I will always remember him. But in addition to dealing with the heartbreak of Tony's death, the original problem remained: Ray Vitale was out for vengeance. His attempts to have Maura disfigured were the disclosure of his inability to ever process the fact that she did not belong to him. I feared for her well-being.

One week after Tony's funeral, I sat at Mary's table with his Colt Revolver in my hands. I talked with Mary as I cleaned the gun. We spoke of Ray Vitale and the pain he had caused her family. We spoke of the threat he posed to Maura and myself. The anger grew so deeply inside me, and I felt compelled to take matters into my own hands. Getting to Ray would not be easy— and, most likely, it would be a suicide mission—but no one who would cause so much pain deserves to live. I expressed that to Mary over and over again. She simply stood up, walked slowly across the room and removed the gun from my hands. She placed it in the wooden case and turned the key to the lock.

"It's not for you to decide, Michael; it's God's will that shall be done, and it will be carried out by the police, not at the hands of a vigilante. You have to rise above the evil to get away from it," she told me wisely.

She had been hurt so badly, she had suffered such a tremendous loss at the hands of one individual, and yet she was the voice of reason. Mary made me realize that my anger should not be my guiding force.

There was still the issue of Maura's safety, and I knew that if we were going to be able to protect her, we had to get her out of town. Mary and I set forth a plan to get Maura to her aunt's home in Scranton, Pennsylvania. My hometown from another time, Scranton, was a coal mining town far enough to the north that Ray Vitale would have no influence there. The town was big enough to get lost in, but nowhere near the size of New York or Philadelphia. It seemed like a good idea, and Maura was in agreement with the exception that her mother must come with her. We packed her clothes that night and headed out of Winchester by the cover of darkness in Tony's old Ford Model A. The next morning, Mary spoke with Alice, Maura's mother, and helped her to make arrangements to be on the afternoon train and to meet us in Scranton when we arrived. It was all very covert as so many people reported to Ray. He had ears everywhere. We were careful that only a select few people knew of our plans, and by the time Ray had realized she left town, there wasn't a single source of reference as to our whereabouts.

Chapter 12

Two hundred thirty-three miles and three long days of mud holes, soaking rain, and overheating radiators later, Maura and I arrived in Scranton, the home I had known in my previous life. It was different In 1928. Scranton was a bustling coal town, alive with culture and prosperity, a mini-New York City in the rolling Pennsylvania hills.

I knew of the dismal days that the little town would have in years to come. One gross miscalculation would cause a coal company to mine beneath the river and, when they got too close to the river bottom, the once-productive coal mines became the path of least resistance. The river flowed freely through the mines, stopping all coal production in the area. It would be a fateful day of death and destruction on January 22, 1959. That one disaster would single-handedly destroy the soul of Scranton and the surrounding areas. The entire valley would fall into a financial depression and never truly recover.

The Scranton of my previous life, the Scranton yet to come, was one of limited industry and opportunity. Scranton of 1928, however, was a different story altogether. It was a booming, bustling city, and Maura and I felt as though we could blend right into its culture.

Since we were hiding out, so to speak, we thought that pursuing our true professions would only make us that much easier to find. We each found employment that would suit our needs of the moment and let us blend in better to the industrial workforce of the town. For the first half of 1928, I followed in the career path of my grandfather and spent my days in the darkness of the coal mines. We were, as they said in the detective novels, on the lam. We were laying low and trying to fit in to keep any word of our whereabouts from getting back to Vitale. He had become obsessed with finding Maura, and she and I were committed to keeping that from ever happening.

It's hard to imagine, but the culture and elegance of the city were virtually unavailable to the average citizen. The wealth remained in the hands of the wealthy. There was always opportunity to let ingenuity and hard work flourish into something, but the average person worked so hard and such long hours that creativity was usually used up just trying to keep your family together, healthy and fed. Although we were in a more prosperous moment for the city itself, we as laborers spent precious little time on endeavors of leisure.

The winter of 1928 was cold and gray. The terrible, gray, overcast clouds, were mixed with the smoke of the coal being burned in every home for as far as the eye could see. The scene was nothing short of dismal. Cold permeated everything, with wind chills to -22 degrees Fahrenheit. Every step out the door was a hat-covered, gloved, layered-clothes drudge from one place to another. It was amazing and by far the coldest, darkest winter I ever remembered; but winter, like our situation, would not last forever.

During the doldrums of that fateful winter, though, we were tasked with learning to endure a true daily grind. Each morning, I would wake up at 5:00am, have coffee with

Maura and her mom in their tiny apartment, then head to the basement to shovel coal onto the grate that sat atop a 55-gallon drum, and I sifted the smaller pieces fit for burning. The drum then fed the coal into the furnace and water heater as needed throughout the day. Then, we bundled up and walked the 10 blocks to Dupree Street, where Maura went to work, sewing in the clothing factory. Hour after hour, she sewed, meeting her quotas in an environment that was akin to a sweatshop, aside from the freezing temperatures. Day in and day out, she did her part to help keep us afloat.

After leaving Maura each morning, I climbed the hill out to the east of town to the mine entrance. I started at 7:00am and ended my day at 7:00pm, every bit of every day was a struggle. The freezing temperatures above ground made no difference to the mines below. The average temperature in the mine was 54°, but the machinery and the gases would raise the temperature to upwards of 100°F. In the middle of the coldest winter on record, I spent the days sweating through my clothes as my cohorts and I picked and shoveled our way through the mines 300 feet below the Earth. We were guided only by headlamps through water, six to 12 inches deep, as we set charges and exploded through to the most abundant natural resources of our time.

Every day, every single day, was spent in a test of will just to survive in an industry that was thriving on the backs of people living just one notch above slavery. We were paid in tokens that were only good at the company store. We were free to leave if we wished. However, tokens never went quite far enough and the debts to the company store could accrue rapidly if one were supporting a family. Those debts were passed on to the wife and children of the miners when they passed away. Limited opportunity for progress and mounting debts very nearly committed a person to a life of mining. The time I spent as a Pennsylvania coal miner counted me among the men who gave everything they had just to stay alive. They were smart and strong and adaptable, a breed of their own. The life of a coal miner was both harsh and volatile.

I realized the tenacity of my future bride one cold night in March when the boiler went out and the temperatures throughout our coal-driven, steam-heated home dropped in next to no time. I went out back and chopped a wheelbarrow full of wood. In a few minutes, the fireplace roared, heating the living room for Maura and myself. Alice had gone to her sister's to stay warm, but my wife-to-be embraced the challenge by my side as she always did, and we fell asleep on the sofa in each other's arms.

I awoke to the embers glowing and, as I stood to tend the fire, I saw her in the doorway, her long, strawberry-blonde hair flowing elegantly over her shoulders. Her eyes, the most amazing eyes I had ever seen, were as blue as the Caribbean Sea. In those eyes, I saw all that she was: beautiful, kind, loving, passionate. It was a repeat of the moment that started this whole adventure. She was even wearing the same dress as she had been wearing in the apparition. Maura questioned my prolonged gaze. I just brushed it off, saying I was barely awake. For me, that moment solidified my purpose. My quest to be with her had led me to that moment. The vision, or apparition, had become a reality.

I was always a dreamer. In the gloomy, overcast winter, I dreamt of summer days with Maura at the lake. Come to think of it, it was always the thought of her that kept me going. Each night, we sat together on the living room sofa. I would hold her in my arms and we would talk. We would talk for hours of our future, lost in our dreams. The hard work and struggles would disappear, and we would set sail toward those dreams night after night. The present became nothing more than a stepping stone, a launching point for the story of our lives together. Our quest for a better future, getting married and starting a family, kept our thoughts away from the reality of the coal mine. I was ready to settle down.

In the spring of that year, the mining slowed just a little and we did get to enjoy some time off, hiking into the Pennsylvania wilderness. We would set off for the day, on hike after hike, every single Sunday. Nature always had a place in our hearts and the solitude of the woods let us grow together as we enjoyed the natural beauty, just the two of us. We never stalled, never gave up or got caught up in complaining; we merely saw the future as we wanted it to be and kept working toward our goals.

With the money we had brought along from my rather lucrative days as a barnstormer, we were doing well enough. I made some additional side money fixing cars and trucks in our neighborhood. Not everyone had money to pay for my services, and one gentlemen was insistent that I take his old 1922 Indian Scout in exchange for putting a new motor in his truck. I really enjoyed fixing that bike up and I even repainted it, making it the only white-and-gold Indian around.

I was starting to give some thought to opening a motorcycle shop on the edge of town. At first, my excitement grew with the idea of getting out of the mines and spending my days above ground, tending to the maintenance of one of my favorite forms of transportation. I pictured the shop in my mind everyday. I pictured Maura working alongside me and lunches together in the park.

Just as we were about to put our savings into the investment, one of the few historic memories from my former life crashed through, and I remembered the great stock market crash of 1929 and the ensuing depression that followed. The next years were going to be rough, and I knew it in advance. That was what put my dreams of business ownership on hold. The crash would hit and, in an instant, I would be grateful for the security of a dirty-filthy mining job and the money we had stashed beneath the mattress in our apartment. I never used my knowledge of the future to win a bet or increase my wealth in the stock market but merely to protect the interests of my family. I always thought it was a Golden Rule sort of thing. The tremendous dive in the market would, however, provide an opportunity for home ownership, and that was an investment in our future which would benefit us many times over the years that followed.

Chapter 13

Winter lead to spring, and I was starting to feel trapped in my mining job. Initially, that was just a feeling, until one warm April morning came. We headed into the mines together as we did every day, the team of seven with myself as the team lead. It was pre-dawn as our team had agreed to an early start in exchange for an early finish. The morning was quiet and calm. The twinkling stars set against the crisp, black sky hinted toward a beautiful spring day just across the boundary of the dawn.

But that blue sky, that spring day which the clear sky promised, I would never see. As we were descending, the gases were rising to the top of the shaft that housed our ventilation fan. My men and I walked down deeper into the mine, laughing and joking by the light of our headlamps. It all seemed very familiar; nothing felt wrong or out of step. We were just going through our early-morning routine as we descended beneath the earth to start our day. Once established in the area of our day's work, we decided to take a coffee break. The seven of us sat on the tool carts and displaced anthracite, sipping our morning java.

Brrrrr, brroom! BOOOM! The sound was deafening. The earth rumbled beneath our feet and the entire world came crashing in upon us. The ground was quaking and we were within the earth—not a good place to be. We each attempted to stabilize ourselves. I pushed my body up against the wall and clung with all my might while trying to protect my head behind my shoulder.

At first, I saw the light from the headlamps of my crew, and seconds later, giant chunks of coal went flashing by my head. I cringed in the darkness, clinging for all I was worth, praying silently for it all to stop. When the anthracite settled, the dust thickened the air.

I struggled to breathe. It felt as though we were going to suffocate. I hung on in expectation of my death until the noise subsided, and maybe a bit longer, as it took a conscious effort to pry my hands free from the wall of coal. When the dust began to settle around me, I looked in every direction for a sign that the others had survived. In the end, I only saw one other headlamp flickering on and off in the distance.

In the investigation that followed the collapse, a faulty fan was suspected among the possible causes. It was presumed that a loose wire on the giant ventilation device caused it to operate sporadically. The intermittent operation of the fan allowed the gases to build up in the ventilation shaft. The wire sparked as the voltage arced across the loose connector and ignited the gas in an explosion that rattled the earth for miles around. Beneath the surface, our world shook incessantly and mineshaft after mineshaft collapsed in on itself.

Minutes that felt like hours later, the dust began to settle and and that flickering headlamp in the distance was all that I could see. We were trapped, myself and hopefully at least one other person who I presumed was attached to that flickering light. Alone in the darkness with no sense of direction, as calmly as possible, I started to yell over toward the lamp.

"Steve...Mark...Billy....Johnny... George....Shawn?" I said.

No response. I moved cautiously toward the light. As I got to within feet of him, his headlamp stopped flickering and developed a soft glow that illuminated the floating particles of coal that filled the air. The dust was still settling, and I could feel it in every breath I took. I wet my bandana with water from my canteen to construct a makeshift air filter, then I tied it across my mouth and nose.

A small mountain blocked the path to my friend. I started in, moving rocks and coal over and over to get to him. When I arrived, he was unconscious; breathing, but unconscious. Taking the canteen from my belt, I sparingly cupped some water into my hand then splashed his face and gently slapped him to try to bring him around.

It took a few tries, but eventually, he came back to me. Johnny and I sat together as I explained what had happened and I had him check to see if he could move his arms and legs and if he felt any pain. He was fine. Giant chunks of rock and coal encircled his entire body but, by some miracle, he came through it all without a scratch—well, maybe a scratch or two, but unharmed nonetheless.

For some reason, I remember the light from his headlamp glancing across the face of my watch, and I realized it was 8:15am—8:15am on Thursday, the 19th of April.
The hands on my watch at that moment in time were stuck in my head from then on, as it was at that moment I realized we'd lost the other members of our party. Five men were buried alive in an instantaneous collapse, the result of an explosion that should never have happened. They were gone without a trace. The mine swallowed my friends and left their families to deal with the aftermath.

The harsh realities of those days were enough to crush their spirits, but somehow, each of their families would eventually push through. It was uncertain at the time whether or not Johnny and I would ever live beyond the mine ourselves. We sat in the darkness, shouting their names, but no response was ever given. Our voices echoed through the shaft, never to be heard. John clicked on his light.

"They're gone," he mumbled.

I caught a glimpse of him wiping a tear from his eye. In the swipe of his hand, big John went from emotional to stoic, and stoic was where he stayed.

We both realized that we had to keep it together. I remember thinking, *Stay busy*. The military always taught that, in a crisis situation, productivity would stem off panic, and panic was the one thing we could not allow. We had limited light and possibly limited oxygen. We were in for an adventure that no one would ever choose. John assessed our immediate area, summing his findings up in another mumble.

“There's no way out," he said quietly, then he clicked off his light and sat next to me in the darkness.

The constant drip of water off to my right became amplified in my brain. We both came to the realization rather quickly that we needed to stay busy and stay calm. I suggested we take turns beating a large stone against the coal wall, hoping that soon our rescuers would hear us and know that we were alive. Drip click, drip click, drip click, drip click. Sounds echoed in the darkness, a mixture of man-made rhythm and nature’s dripping water from overhead.

It was my turn with the rock. John was sleeping. He dozed off in the middle of the story of his childhood in a small home on the Erie Canal. Exhausted from the events of the day and the lack of food, even my banging had become some sort of soothing rhythm. After a while, alone and left to my thoughts, I started to drift off myself. Drip click, drip click, drip—drip—drip. I awoke again in short order and oscillated between my thoughts and my dreams for a while.

I have always feared a deadly diagnosis from the doctor. My parents both died way too early, and premature death from a heart condition or a stroke was something that lingered beneath the surface of my mind at all times. Somehow, though, trapped beneath the earth, in the darkness of a coal-lined tomb, conceding to death was never a possibility. Instead, I clung to my memories. I had only thoughts of Maura. Maura, that first day at the lake, as she climbed up on the rock with her long hair flowing over her shoulders. Silhouetted by the sun, her appearance was angelic: a sexy, curvaceous angel—my angel. Drip...drip...drip... I peacefully slipped away to my dreams. Drip...drip...drip.

Chapter 14

Drip... drip...drip ...The water dripped rhythmically from her hair. The sun glistened off of her skin and droplets of sunshine warmed her body as she dried in the gentle summer breeze. Drip...drip...drip...She sat upon the rocks. I walked closer to her, trying my best to stay calm, to be cool on my approach.

Drip...drip...drip...The blood ran from her fingertips as she pressed them against the wound in her chest. I looked to her feet; the blood pooled on the rock beneath her! Her lips uttered my name and begged for help. Drip...drip...drip...the lifeblood was leaving her body right before my eyes while I stood helplessly just a few feet away.

"I told you I would have my revenge."

His voice echoed in my head as he stood over her, the gun still smoking in his hand. His eyes were glazed: no smile, no laughter, just a demonized look of determination. He turned and walked away. I reached for her but I could not get to her! Drip...drip...drip ...that horrific little noise in my ears, an overwhelming feeling of helplessness in my heart as I screamed her name and struggled once more to reach her.

"Maura! Maura!" I cried desperately.

My heart was racing, my head in a fog, when I opened my eyes to the pitch-black darkness of the mine. Drip...drip...drip...the water from above dripped into the puddle at my feet. Unknowingly, she may have saved my life in that moment.

After my nightmare, I realized that, no matter what, I had to get out of that mine. She wasn't safe. She would never be safe as long as he lived. I had to get out of that mine to be there for her. I had to protect her. I had to end his threats to her, his threats to us. In that moment of waking to the darkness, my resolve replaced my submission. I was going to fight with every last breath to find a way out, to find my way back to her side.

Chapter 15

I doubled my efforts in looking for some sign of weakness in the walls and floor of the mine. It was a ridiculous thought, but I had to exhaust any possibility. In my quest I felt a thin crack, maybe an eighth of an inch thick that ran the distance from the ceiling to the floor. I could feel air flowing rapidly through the crack, a differential in pressure creating some sort of flow. It was good, clean air. We took turns placing our mouths to the crack and sucking in the fresh air. At least we would not suffocate. We tried to yell for help, but no one ever responded. Crack or no crack, no one could hear us. Day two passed much the same way as day one had: darkness, hunger, thirst, nightmares, darkness, darkness and more darkness. The crack provided air, but air adapts to all sorts of curves, rises and dips. There was no real weakness in our tomb. It was all to no avail.

We started our third day with our rations completely depleted. We had survived thus far on the remnants of lunchpails and coffee thermoses; two of each had ended up in our vicinity. The little bit of water we had brought down with us was nearly gone. The continuous drip was soon to become a source of hydration. We took turns leaving our canteens beneath that drip for hours on end just to get a few swigs of water. Big John fell asleep in his corner again, and I stared off into a darkness the likes of which you cannot imagine. The task, it seemed, was to wait for rescue and not lose your mind in the process.

I once knew of a group of four men who had been trapped for a week in a cabin after an avalanche in the Swiss Alps. They all survived, but no one would talk about it. Each time they were asked, they simply stated that hunger does strange things. I imagined that they'd been sizing up the smallest guy for dinner if they didn't get rescued soon.

In this case, I was the smallest guy. I listened to Big John's snoring yet again; he didn't seem to have the energy or desire to turn me into barbecue. Then again, hunger does strange things. The hunger pains would ebb and flow and they had subsided for the moment as I sat, staring into the darkness, praying for salvation, thinking of how nice it had felt just to hold Maura's hand in mine.

Far above us, on the surface, the argument had arisen that the chance that we were still alive was minimal. Only two men and one woman held out any hope. Maura would never give up. She spoke with every engineer, every manager, even the owner of the mine, trying to be sure that they continued their rescue attempt. Big John's best friends, two brothers, Eric and Shamus Flynn, completed the trio. They were the only three people who would not give up.

Eric, Shamus and Maura dug alongside two teams in an effort that went on day and night in order to bring us back. Maura was not some screaming girlfriend, just begging for help. She was, in fact, the voice of reason that spoke on our behalf in a calm, cool, collected tone about the value of our lives and the need for the crews to go on. She was persuasive and confident, and as a result, those in charge of the mine never stopped trying to provide us with a means of escape. If there was any way, a one-in-a-million shot, they were going to try. The crews got behind her. They knew in their hearts it could very well have been them. It was not a matter of logic; it was a matter of humanity. "No miner left behind" became the sentiment.

The crews dug through two different blockages to get to the main shaft that would allow access to where we had been digging. Fifty feet after the second blockage, they faced a wall of granite that they knew could not be moved. The only solution was to drill and blast their way through. It was risky and would be very dangerous, at least to John and myself, but from their end, all other options had been depleted. Due to its position in the upper part of the shaft, they felt confident that the large, granite boulder which was blocking the path would not be in our immediate vicinity. They were right; we were, in fact, much further beneath the earth. That boulder had to go, and blasting was the only way to remove it in a timely manner that would offer us even a chance of survival. The decision was made to blast the granite.

Maura was an asset to the fight. Her involvement made her feel as though she was a part of the solution rather than a victim of circumstance. However, in the evenings, when things would slow down, her fears could no longer be suppressed and she would cry alone in her room. With each passing hour, hope was fading, but her determination was the impetus for the duration of the rescue efforts.

It was the morning of day four, or so I estimated, John was no longer conscious. I could hear his shallow breathing, but I could not get him to speak to me. There was no chance of him killing me for sustenance, as far as I could tell. I opened my eyes for no good reason. When it is that dark, wakefulness and sleep are merely the differentiation between your eyes being closed and being open. My eyelids were open as I sat in silence, listening again to that constant drip... drip... drip.. It was like an hourglass dripping the sands of time away—each drip a second; each drip a second closer to death. I shook off the morbid thoughts and sent my mind to the days at the lake. Stay Sane Until Rescue was my only mission; my mind was my only weapon.

From where we sat, it was a muffled explosion, dynamite in the distance; but it brought a moment of hope. Big John awoke, and we both felt the energy of that hopefulness for what had to be a good 30 or 40 seconds. Then we felt the rumble. The whole mine began to shake again as we clung once more to the walls. We were going to be crushed by the rescue efforts, after all. I never wanted to die in fear, but I couldn't help it; I was scared. I started to literally see my whole life flash before my eyes. It seemed like an eternity, but in less than a minute, the quaking earth gave way once more to calm, calm, quiet darkness. No lamplight left. Nothing for us to see. In my ears I heard it again: drip... drip... drip... If I wasn't so dehydrated, I probably would have cried.

The drip suddenly stopped. I put my hand beneath the area where it had been and felt the water streaming. It started off as a trickle, but the stream of water grew rapidly. In minutes, it was splashing on the floor like a running faucet. A second stream started from my left. The water began to stream from every side of the ceiling, voraciously filling the shaft. What a horrible way to die. I felt the cold on my ankles and later my knees, then the water surpassed my waist.

"Mikey, I can't swim!" Big John yelled across to me.

There was nowhere to swim to, I thought to myself. We were both overwhelmed. Adrenaline surged through my body, fight or flight, with nowhere to go. The sound reminded me of being beneath the falls at Niagara. The water soon reached my mouth and I took one last gulp of air.

A muffled crumbling above my head was the last thing I heard. The ceiling of the mine gave way above me and about five feet to my left. In the rush of water, I felt my body tumbling and twisting, churning with the massive flow from above. The water settled quickly when the shaft was fully submerged, and I hung there for a second, floating in the cold, dark abyss.

Above the surface, Maura and the engineers watched helplessly as the anthracite filled the opening to the mine. As strong as she had been, she turned away, crushed from within. There was simply no hope. The blast had caused a secondary disaster from which there would be no recovery. She walked home alone, silently climbing the stairs toward her room. Alice met her in the hallway, knowing in a glance her daughter's pain. They wept openly in each other's arms.

In that cold, dark, wet abyss, I was unable to tell which way was up. With my final effort, unsure of the outcome, I expelled some of that last precious breath and floated toward the roof of the mine. My left hand felt an opening, a large opening. Desperate for air, I reached in every direction hoping to find big John and take him with me. It was to no avail. In the darkness and running out of air, I had no choice but to thrust my body in the direction that I assumed was up. A light shimmered in the distance and I swam upward toward it.

I broke through to the surface with a gasp. The light blinded me as my head pierced the surface of the underground lake and I rolled onto my back, just barely keeping my mouth above water, with some distorted rendition of the backstroke.

It was actually painful after days of darkness even with my eyes closed. I couldn't take it, so I rolled to my stomach and began to doggy paddle.

I had no energy left, but my body moved on instinct, propelled purely by the fear of drowning. When I forced my eyes open again, a beam of sunlight piercing the ceiling of the cavern illuminated a shore of stone. My squinting gave way to an acceptance of the light, and I paddled my body slowly in the direction of that shore. The light was distant, probably 200 feet above my head. There was no real hope of ever getting out through that hole, which led to the side of a mountain 10 miles from the nearest person, place or thing, but the light brought my smile as I slowly worked my way to the rocky edge of the underground lake.

Cold, wet and exhausted, still far beneath Earth's surface, I clawed and crawled my way through the last few feet of shallow water to dry land. As the sun moved across the sky, it aligned with the hole in the earth above me and shined upon my body. Too exhausted to move, I laid there, thankful for the bit of warmth that it delivered, and my eyes closed once more. Exhaustion was victorious. I fell asleep.

Chapter 16

Patrick Flannery was a warrior at heart. A marine during World War I, he had seen battle firsthand. At six feet, four inches tall and 210 pounds of solid muscle, Patrick was a force of nature. He was a lean, muscular and athletic man. His wife Carolyn was his perfect compliment: tall, strong and slender and an athlete in her own right with the heart of an angel. It was that angelic heart that had saved Pat from a far darker path in life, and he lived in gratitude to his wife for showing him the way to the light and bestowing upon him the faith by which he lived.

Before the children, they would spend their evenings running together around the lake and their weekends off on epic treks throughout the nearby woods. Their two daughters, Bridgette and Molly, followed in their footsteps. The entire family was adventurous. Weekend campouts were filled with long hikes in the woods, climbing the sheer rock faces of the local landscape and repelling into the natural caves hidden in the mountains of northeastern Pennsylvania.

Ever since Patrick was a child, he enjoyed spelunking. In his younger years, he and his friends would explore abandoned mines and caves throughout the mountains. In the spring of 1928, Patrick, in his 40s, along with Carolyn and their teenage daughters, was repeating and expanding upon the endeavors of his youth.

One fateful morning in April of 1928, their family set out on an adventure that would save my life. Had it not been for Patrick and his rather unique entourage, my little nap by the underground lake may have become my final sleep. Fortunately for me, the Flannerys had decided that, on that particular day of their camping trip, they would go out together and explore one particular cave from Pat's memory.

I never heard them as they slid down the rope or yelled to one another across the cavern. Each one took their turn to see who would let go from the highest point and make the biggest splash. The water rippled against my ankles as they splashed back and forth, but I didn't feel a thing. I never saw Molly swimming toward me as she set out on her quest to find some new and interesting rocks for her collection. I was oblivious to the concern on the little girl's face, and even the sound of her frightened voice, as she yelled to her parents for help when she came upon my near-lifeless body lying on the shore. My only memories of those moments were glimpses of light and faces, then darkness once again.

It was young Molly who relayed the story to me in my hospital bed when the Flannerys came to visit. Evidently, I struggled, coming in and out of consciousness as Pat carried me to the point where the rope touched the water. Carolyn and the girls had made a makeshift float from a backpack that supported my head as I lay beneath the rope. Then Pat shimmied up to the opening, followed by the girls. Carolyn stayed behind, watching over me, and eventually fashioning a harness with the rope once the others were safely through the opening.

With all his might, Pat pulled my body through to the light of day. The girls stabilized me as Pat untied the rope and sent it back for Carolyn. In another flash of memory through my faded consciousness, Pat assured me that I was going to be all right, that he would get me to safety.

Together, they created a stretcher from some fallen trees and vines. Before nightfall, they all carried me to the safety of their home. The ambulance took me from there to the hospital and my mining career came to its official end. It was nothing short of a miracle that I had survived, and the efforts of the Flannery family were nothing less than heroic—heroes, each and every one of them. I didn't remember much, just glimpses of their kindness. Little Molly's stories were what filled in the gaps.

Maura arrived at the hospital just as the sirens from the ambulance fell silent. She was at my side before I ever reached the doors. My consciousness waned, but I knew she was there. She was with me. I felt her hand in mine. When I awoke in my hospital bed eight hours later, there was an I.V. in my arm. Maura's hand was still in mine; she never left my side.

Seeing that I was awake, she stood up and hugged me. She held me like she would never let me go. In that moment, I felt every feeling a man could have: grief, for the loss of six of my friends; fear, for narrowly escaping the end of my life; love, love so intense that it made my tattered body feel whole again; gratitude, grateful for the second chance at life I had been given. Tears welled in my eyes and in hers. We had come so close to it ending before it really got started.

Every muscle in my body was weakened from nearly starving to death. My left leg was bruised and battered and somehow I had sprained my ankle during my final struggle toward the surface. Maura never left my side during the weeks of my recovery. She encouraged me every step of the way, laughing with me and struggling with me, as my body learned to eat again, to walk, to run. It was a rebirth for me. Emerging from the darkness of the mine was the best man that I could possibly be. I would learn to live and love to a degree that I never even knew was possible.

For years I had heard the phrase, "Perception is reality." My reality ran through a filter of nearly bringing my life to a cold, dark and starving ending. Darkness and impending death brightened every bit of everything in my life from that point forward.

My relationship with Maura was stronger than ever. She accompanied me to the memorial service for big John and the rest of our crew. Not one other body had been recovered, not even John's. By some miracle, I had survived when six others had perished, and that fact weighed heavily on my heart. I missed my friends and coworkers every day. I wished that there was some way that they could have survived, some way that that their families would not have known the anguish of such loss. Maura shared in my sadness; she nurtured the wounds of my soul with her kindness and understanding.

Maura was the guiding force of my recovery. We went for hike after hike through the woods. Ricketts Glen State Park became my own personal rehab facility, strengthening my lungs and my legs in its natural beauty. We ran the trails, shaded in the oak and hemlock trees, together. We scaled the paths along the falls with our hearts pounding and our lungs filling with the cool, moist air along the water's edge.

I was on a mission to get my life started again. We were up and running at full steam with the wedding just months away. We only had two problems. One was my lack of employment: I had promised Maura that I would not return to work in the coal mines, and truth be told, I had no desire to ever see the anthracite labyrinth again. Our second problem was the forever-looming thought that we would be found out, that Ray Vitale would somehow catch up to us and exact a vengeance of death and destruction.

After saving my life, Patrick Flannery became one of the best friends that I would ever have. Every morning before my hikes with Maura, Pat and I would run the lake, then he would join me in practicing some of the martial arts techniques that I had learned in my previous life. That martial arts training centered me, and I believe Pat always enjoyed it as well.

Our friendship grew throughout my recovery and, when I was ready, it was Pat who solved the first of our two problems. On one of our Thursday night dinners with him and Carolyn, Pat asked if I would come to work with him at the railroad. If he had been expecting any hesitance in my response, he got none—I jumped on the chance to earn a steady paycheck. Carolyn warned me of the dangers; the railroads were not much safer than the mines. I was just happy that the work was above ground. Her concern was justified, but I knew that if I kept my head about me I could avoid the hazards and make a good wage for a day's work.

Chapter 17

I started working at the Coxton Yard railroad facility on June 1, 1928. I learned my way around the operations of the switching yard rather quickly, thanks to Pat. While it was indeed another dangerous job, diligence and training limited my exposure to risk. Much like flying, good planning and standard operating procedures were the best way to minimize that risk. At the rail yard, though, with such massive machinery in motion at every turn, an excessive element of risk always remained, and it was ultimately the experience of my veteran coworkers that kept us all safe. We would operate according to need, and man power was limited, which often led to long, hard days. I was happy, though—I was above ground, working in the sunshine and meeting new challenges with a good friend along to guide my way.

June 22nd had been one of those rather long days of work for me. Right around 6:30pm, as I approached my 10th hour of a double shift, Marco replaced me while I took my dinner break. I went down to the sports field next to the rail yard. Pat and I would meet on the east side of that field every day to work out on the makeshift strength training equipment that he had designed. He was always developing new ways to push himself and he had read a newspaper article on the training men endured for a strongman competition in New York City. The article inspired my inquisitive friend, and I joined him daily in a routine that was, at the time, a novelty.

The weight training and running were all a part of Pat's philosophy of life: train the machine, keep the vehicle—your body—strong. He never wanted to be limited in what he was capable of doing. As he said, most of the amazing sights in this world are off the beaten path. Only a strong, healthy body can get you to them.

On that afternoon, we were using an old set of railroad pump car wheels and an axle as a barbell for bench presses when I first heard an airplane in the distance. It seemed far off in the larger part of the valley. It approached from the southwest, and then the sound faded as it moved eastward. I remember thinking that I hoped the aviator was familiar with the area, as the distant mountains were covered in fog. We went back to our weight training without giving any additional thought to the airplane.

Working out with Pat was a humbling experience, but he was always lighthearted and his joking around made it anything but competitive. We had finished our strength training for the day and were sitting together, eating dinner from our lunch pails. Pat sat on the bench, and I perched myself atop an old truck tire. The evening sun was descending above the fog layer. Its brightness made me squint while we spoke. I found it distracting, so distracting that I never even heard him as he approached.

The lone eagle flew along the river southwest of Wilkes-Barre, threading through the mountain passes until the valley opened up below him. A turn toward the east would put him on course for his destination, New York City. He strained his eyes, peering off into the distance in an attempt to find an opening in the fog bank.

There was no opening to be found. He made his way north and then south again along the ridge. The low-hanging clouds appeared impenetrable across the eastern hills. He tried once more to no avail, then in defeat, he returned to the river, his source of navigation, in quest of a small local airfield. He was unshaken; there were still plenty of options for the experienced aviator to resolve his dilemma. He reoriented himself with his map and turned to the north at the Y in the river. The clouds once more blocked his way as he made the turn. Trapped within the valley, he circled back, looking in earnest for a place to set down. The little airport would not be in the cards; he needed a field, some flat piece of land. But then, beneath him, he saw a rail yard, then the sports field. It looked good: with soft, short grass and plenty of room. A smile spread across his face as he made his approach from the east.

I was startled and instinctively ducked my head when the large, black tires soared just a few feet above us. With the throttle at idle, the propeller loafed around quietly as the large silver, wings darkened the evening sky and the pilot eased the monoplane to a gentle touchdown not more than

100 feet from us on the soft grass of the sports field. It was as nice as any airfield I had ever used, but I'd never really seen it as such prior to his landing.

The airplane taxied to the far end of the field then turned sideways as he cut the engine and the propeller clanked to a stop. I couldn't believe it; I was in awe. I recognized it at once. The silver Ryan Brougham was being flown around the country by no other than Charles Lindbergh in an effort to promote aviation. I had been following his endeavors in the newspaper.

It looked a lot like its predecessor, the Spirit of St. Louis, which Lindbergh had flown to become the first man to fly solo across the Atlantic. The main difference was the addition of a bank of windows across the front that replaced the periscope viewing system. The door eased open and the lanky pilot unfolded himself from the cockpit, holding his map in his right hand. Charles Lindbergh himself stepped toward us as Pat and I ran to meet him.

To say that we were amazed would be an understatement. In a rather dry and authoritative tone, young Mr. Lindbergh informed us that there was nothing to be alarmed about. He had merely chosen the Coxton Rail Yard as a safe place to let down for a while and let the weather clear. Evidently, the clouds had kept getting lower and lower as he'd pressed on toward the east. He turned back in search of a small airfield northwest of Scranton, but again, the weather would prohibit his progress. Seeing the sports field next to the railyard, Mr. Lindbergh decided that it was far more prudent to settle in on the soft grass and wait for the weather to improve. He had a coffee with us and shared the trials and tribulations of his latest endeavor: flying across the country promoting aviation and the value it would have to local communities. We were blown away by the unexpected arrival of one of the most famous men in the world.

It wasn't long before the press started to arrive. Shortly after that, throngs of people came out to see the celebrity. Mr. Lindbergh spoke briefly to the crowd, then at the request of one of the railroad engineers, he waved goodbye as he set off to accept his offer of a train ride. Newspaper reports said that

Charles Lindbergh truly enjoyed his opportunity to pilot the large locomotive for a brief stint that evening; the engineer had let old Lucky Lindy take the controls.

When they returned, Pat asked me to take our guest out through the north entrance of the rail yard and bring him back to my house while he sent the press off in another direction in order to protect his privacy. The press believed that Mr. Lindbergh would be spending the evening at the local YMCA. We even had one of our guys stop by and sign the registry for him.

That night, Maura outdid herself. We ate a fantastic steak and potato smorgasbord in our little apartment with literally the most famous aviator of all time. The entire experience was surreal. They say you should never meet your heroes, that they will only disappoint you. That was not the case with Mr. Lindbergh. He was the real deal, a genuine American hero with a heart of gold and the straightforward, honest approach to life that made you forget his celebrity status altogether.

He and I shared coffee and dessert in the living room, listening to radio reports of his landing at the local rail yard and the statements of those at the scene. He said he never understood the whole celebrity thing and that he always tried to keep it from getting in the way. No one spoke of where Charles was at the moment, and the suspense added to the excitement for the local press. I talked with him of my barnstorming experience in the Eaglerock. It was a lifestyle I knew he was intimately familiar with, for he himself had been a barnstormer before he became an airmail pilot. He loosened up a bit when he realized that he was among friends and that aviation had been such a large part of our lives as well. He told us first hand of his experience flying solo across the Atlantic. In 1927, that was the equivalent of going to the moon. No other man had completed a solo crossing prior. He told us of the frozen compass that led him to pure, old-fashioned Northstar over my shoulder—celestial navigation.

He spoke of spirits and apparitions that he wasn't sure should be spoken of or attributed to exhaustion. He told us of the young boy waving madly on the shore of Ireland, and of the relief he felt at the sight of land. He spoke of the beauty of Paris at night, and how the City of Light welcomed him, boosting his spirits after over 33 hours in the air. His triumphant arrival in France filled the city with excitement, and the energy of the crowds was endearing, even though they nearly tore his plane to bits in search of a momento. He was riveting and precise in his descriptions of the event that changed the world and his life forever.

The next morning Mr. Lindbergh wanted to leave early, so I drove him back to the rail yard, where I would return to work. On the ride in, Charles offered me a job. He stated that he was to be working with Juan Trippe of Pan American Airways, scouting out efficient, safe routing for commercial passenger service as well as airmail routes throughout South America and the Caribbean. It all started in the Caribbean and South America, but it would eventually encompass the world. He said he needed a few good pilots to work as scouts, flying light airplanes to scope out those routes for future airline service.

Charles asked if I would be willing to join his team of aviators. The pay was four times what I was making at the rail yard, and I would have the opportunity to be a part of something big, something that would change the way the world would travel forever. I could return to my love of flying and, eventually, to the same career I had in my future/past. It was a tremendous offer, and before he stepped out of the truck I agreed to talk it over with Maura. He left me his phone number and address and asked that I let him know as soon as possible.

I helped Lindbergh untie his plane and ready it for flight. It really was a beautiful machine; Ryan made some nice airplanes in 1928. At 5:45am, as the morning sun rose in the east, I spun the propeller of the little Wright engine and brought it to life. He was airborne in minutes, and I offered a wave from the field below that was more of a salute to my new friend. His early start avoided the majority of the crowds while he got underway to New York once more.

Not more than two hours later, though, we heard him approaching again from the east. The fog and rolling hills had once again impeded his progress and he returned to safe haven, landing again at Coxton Yard. With a second chance to meet the legend, people came from all over to the little sports field. Local dignitaries talked him into a luncheon in his honor in the nearby small town of Pittston. Shortly after lunch, around 1:30pm, Charles Lindbergh disappeared once more over the hills on the eastern horizon. The lone aviator made his way safely to New York City that day with views of rolling, green hills and crystal-clear lakes that rippled in the sunshine as the fog had finally given way to clear, blue summer skies.

When I returned to work that day, keeping Lindbergh's offer to myself was difficult but necessary. I felt that Maura should be the first person I told. I just kept smiling and letting my thoughts run to exotic Island destinations with Maura at my side. With another day of rail yard work behind me, I was glad to see that the barber shop was opened a little later that Friday evening. I could get a clean shave, take Maura to the amusement park for a few rides on the rollercoaster, and then for dinner before I asked her two very important questions.

When I stepped in the door of his shop, little Nick was playing with a toy car on the floor while his father finished clipping Mr. Rosetti from the apartment next to ours. Everyone shared a few minutes of mumbled greetings. I picked up the paper, then I sat in the chair to peruse the headlines. Mr. Rosetti spoke first.

"That reporter fella in the nice suit ever get a hold of you, Mike?" he asked me.

"No, what reporter?" I responded.

Mr. Rosetti went on to explain the details of his encounter that day with a gentlemen from the Times who was interested in speaking with me. He said the guy wanted my angle on the Lindbergh landing since I was a pilot and the world's most noted aviator had just landed at my place of employment. I told Mr. Rosetti that I hadn't heard from anyone. He just shrugged and asked when it was that I flew airplanes. I made light of it, saying that it was during the war and left it at that. A lot of men kept their war stories to themselves, and it was common courtesy not to pry into those areas of a man's life.

Again, looking back, everything is crystal clear. I had never shared my flying with a single soul in the Scranton area. If that man had actually been a reporter, he couldn't have known about my background in aviation. The notably sharp suit, the extra information—they were all indicators of who the inquisitive mystery man actually was. It never dawned on me at the time. I wish it had.

When Mr. Rosetti left, the bell rang above the door, and I sat in the chair to take my turn at a trim and the cleanest shave a man could get. I wanted to look good.

Chapter 18

That evening, Maura and I boarded the Laurel Line train to Rocky Glen Park. The park had started as a mere picnic area along a creek, but the owner promptly dammed that creek, making it into Rocky Glen Lake. The picnic area blossomed as well into a full-blown amusement park, complete with Maura's favorite ride, the wooden roller coaster. Like so many residents of the nearby cities and townships, we took the train along a short route through the woods that was really a treat in itself. The powerful locomotive gave us a tour of the local area that was unmatched in its natural beauty.

In just over twenty minutes, we were clanking and coasting our way through the first half of the evening. Following our stomach-churning adventure, my smiling fiance and I grabbed a few hamburgers and hotdogs, and then we headed down to the lakeside for a quick dinner. We sat on the rocks near the lake where we met a friend of mine from the rail yard, Dave Robertson. He sat next to us with his wife while his kids frolicked on the lake's shallow edge. I had

Lindbergh's offer on my mind. Ironically, Dave spoke of how he was so locked into the railroad. Dave would say how he was born and raised a railroad man and that he would probably die a railroad man as well. Little did he know, he was only two days away from the death he had so nonchalantly predicted.

When Dave and Susie stepped away to play on the sandy beach with their children, I started speaking to my future wife about the life we were in and the road we were on. While aviation was in its infancy and still far more dangerous than it would be in years to come, the other professions that were prevalent in that day were nearly just as dangerous.

To me, however, the real concern of being involved with the railroad for the remainder of our days was the death of our dreams. It was the idea that we would get so involved in making a living that we would stop making a life. Our lives would be running us and, over time, our dreams would start to die. I felt an overwhelming sadness just thinking about it.

In those thoughts, we were mourning the death of our dreams.

At the root of it, I was from a different time. In my day, the past/future, we were dreamers—the dreamers who made their way through the days and nights of suffering by holding their dreams in their hearts, for once you have a dream, the trials and tribulations of everyday life become nothing more than bumps in the road. The key was to nurture the flame when it was flickering and to live a life filled with choices that kept your dream alive.

I grew up in the kind of America that put an American flag on the moon, an achievement that seemed impossible when Kennedy announced his intentions in 1961. The lunar landing made dreamers of an entire generation. We knew there would be challenges, but, as John Kennedy said, "We do these things not because they are easy, but because they are hard."

That was the attitude of my generation. We believed that you found your passion and followed it, that determination and drive would overcome the obstacles in life and that every day was a step closer to your goals. The security of the rail yard job had a price. That security would be paid for with my very soul. I wanted nothing to do with a life devoid of dreams. People of the time just dutifully trotted along. Life ran the show, people just ran along as best they could. At the time, the railroad seemed to be a secure job that I could return to for many years to come. I was, however, unwilling to pay the price for that supposed security.

As we sat on the lakeside rocks, Maura and I spoke of life and of the importance of always keeping a little adventure in it to make you feel alive. I told her of my feelings toward keeping our dreams alive and the importance of that in the way I wanted to live our life together.

We spoke of the fact that life was just dangerous, no matter what you did for a living in 1928. A man could die flying, or in a coal mine, or at a rail yard. The important thing was not to try to hide from life, but to embrace it. “Let go and let God,” as the saying goes. It was with that thought and a gentle hug that we united into an agreement that our life would be lived and we would never be paralyzed by our fears.

I told her of the job offer that Mr. Lindbergh had put forth. At first, she was taken aback, and I could see the tears welling within her eyes, her initial reaction was fear. Courage is not the absence of fear, but rather the ability to overcome it. The more we spoke, the more she realized that this was not just an opportunity for me—it was, in fact, an opportunity for us. We decided together that we would move up the wedding, answering my first question, and that we would start work as an intrepid, flying couple, exploring the Caribbean and South America together from the cockpit of an airplane.

During that time, it was very uncommon for a woman to be involved in such a dangerous profession. Within the year, however, Anne Morrow Lindbergh would be doing exactly the same thing at the side of Charles. She wrote several great books that referenced this period in her life. Anne's decision to accompany Charles may have been based on Maura's decision to accompany me as we had been a topic of discussion for more than a few nights in their home. I had already taught Maura how to fly during our couples barnstorming exploits the previous summer, and with just a little brushing up, we would both be ready.

While this endeavor would take us to many new lands and different cultures, it would also keep us far, far away from Ray Vitale or any of his men. By the time we ended the discussion, Maura was excited to a level that matched my own. We were going to leave the railroad behind and, with my new salary, we could find a place of our own that suited us. Warm winters and palm trees came to mind, maybe even a beachfront property. We committed to an extraordinary life that day. With her by my side, I felt once again alive and in pursuit of our dreams. Once we established ourselves, we could build a home, have our children and live in peace together.

That night, Charles had called to thank us for our hospitality and I informed him of our decision to take the job and our desire to start within the month. When I told him of Maura's decision to fly along with me, he didn't say much.

"Yeah, sure; that sounds fine," he replied, in his typical tone—dry and brief.

The month would give us plenty of time to finalize the plans and have a small, family wedding, which we felt more than ready for. Once again, it felt as though everything was moving in the right direction, and it was—for a while.

We were married two weeks later in a beautiful French manor in the small town of Sterling, just outside of Scranton. It was a joyful celebration of family and friends; even Mary made the trip from Virginia via train for our weekend gathering.

Maura and her mom drove the old Model T pickup to the wedding. I rode to my big day on my freshly-restored 1922 Indian motorcycle. It was a relic when I first received it. When I was finished, though, the old Indian looked and ran like new. Its white paint with gold trim shined in the morning sun as I raced along the country roads in my new suit and tie. I imagine it was a strange sight with the dust rising in my wake: I was a man on a mission, dressed to the nines.

I arrived early to the wedding and took a few minutes to freshen up, then I headed to meet the priest at the gazebo in the meadow next to the manor. Standing there, I was filled with anticipation—no doubt or fear, just anticipation—to finally be joined with the woman who I had travelled through time for. When I saw Maura walking down the aisle, a song that was yet to be created, a Frank Sinatra tune called "The Way You Look Tonight," filled my thoughts, and I felt like the luckiest man alive. Our celebration lasted until the later hours of the afternoon, when Maura and I headed off to our honeymoon on the old Indian motorcycle. We would never be much of a conventional couple.

We rode off to the old fire road that bounced and bobbled us to the top of East Mountain and a small hunting cabin that Pat let us use. The cabin came complete with an easterly view of the valley that can best be described as spectacular. Our poor man's honeymoon suited us just fine. We were in love in the natural beauty and seclusion of the summer hills.

That night, the sky couldn't have been any more clear, the moon shining like a lantern hung just for us, as we set off to bathe in the small waterfall just a short walk from our cabin. Clean and refreshed, Maura went ahead of me to the cabin in what I thought was a rather strange dash of modesty. She was gone before I even stopped soaking my head in the shower-like spray of the falls.

I slipped on my blue jeans and walked with caution along the path that returned me to our honeymoon suite. My wife was awaiting my return with two sleeping bags lain out next to the glowing embers of what was our fire. The large stone acted like a patio, with an unbelievable view of the stars that I did not see.

Every ounce of my attention was on my new bride standing in front of me with the rising moon behind her, her silk negligee so transparent that it nearly disappeared in that light. Long, flowing hair and enticing curves set against the rising moon made the rest of the universe disappear.

When I kissed her lips, our hearts raced together. They pounded so hard against our chests I was sure they would explode. The passion started to rise. As my hands glided across her silk-covered body, each kiss grew deeper, longer and more passionate than the last. Every touch was electric. I held her tiny waist in my hands and kissed her again. I was completely consumed with desire for my new wife.

I felt the heat of her body, the passion rising within her. Overwhelmed with feelings of love, I brushed back her hair and caressed her shoulders with the back of my fingers as I kissed her neck. My hands rotated inward and, in one smooth motion, my thumbs slid the straps of her lingerie off to the sides, releasing her beautiful body from its silken confines. Naked together, beneath the summer moon, I laid her gently upon the sleeping bags and we made love for the first time, beneath a sea of stars, alone together, at the top of the world.

We had to return on Sunday night from our private mountain retreat as we both had work on Monday morning. Monday through Thursday, work was uneventful; they were just standard days at the yard. That Friday, my last day on the job, I left for work a few hours earlier than usual to help with coverage for a busy spurt inspired by a brief increase in demand for coal, which in turn increased the demand for transportation of that energy source.

I was as happy as I had ever been in my life. I was going to finish my final week at the rail yard and, together, my new wife and I were headed off into an adventurous life that would free us of the worries we had faced from the onset of our time together. Those were my thoughts as I kissed my new wife and headed off to work before breakfast.

Chapter 19

Maura never saw him. His darkened figure had ducked beneath the window as he climbed the stairs to our second-floor apartment. His cohort followed his silent lead. Dressed for work, she went to the kitchen to make herself an egg and oatmeal breakfast. She heated the pan and set a small slab of butter in it that started to melt immediately, then she turned to the icebox to retrieve her eggs. When the door flew open, they expected a scream and a cowering woman who fearfully submitted to their request to vacate her home and accept their offer of an escort to the home of Mr. Vitale.

The first man entered unexpectedly and, in seconds, Maura greeted him with a lunge toward his face. The five-foot-three-inch ball of fire blinded her first assailant by crushing two fresh eggs into his eyes. She was not going peacefully—not a chance. She slid to the side just as the second goon came through her door.

I believe that, for the rest of his life, he wore the scars from the heated cast iron frying pan that she hit him with. He dropped to the floor, unconscious before he could feel the pain. Recovered from his egg encounter, Vinny stepped toward her again. She stepped in his direction then her right foot kicked him so hard that he gasped for air as he fell to his knees.

When she turned to check on goon number two, she heard the gun go off. Looking back, she saw Vinny aiming directly at her.

"Don't make me shoot you," he said.

He stood slowly and gave my wife an armed escort to the running car that awaited them in the street. Two more men ascended the stairs to reclaim their unconscious friend, who had been taken out by a 110-pound little girl. The two plain black sedans sped off beneath the streetlights and started their journey south.

Alice was awakened by the ruckus, but by the time she ascended the stairs, her daughter had been taken. She immediately called the police and then the rail yard.
It took awhile for me to get the message, but as soon as I did, I sprinted to my truck and sped off, raising clouds of dust that billowed in the morning sun. Pat saw my expedient departure and asked what was going on. Before the foreman even finished speaking, Pat was racing out of the parking area himself.

When I got to the house, the police were there, studying the scene. They questioned me, and I told them of the threats Vitale had made and the reason we had fled to the Scranton area. The conversations continued for a bit, and I was getting anxious. The longer we spoke, the further away they got. It was 1928, and the tools at the disposal of the localized police forces were far more limited than they are today. It wasn't just a radio call and an all-points bulletin to get the word out and have the world on alert. It would take a lot more to locate a missing, or in this case kidnapped, person.

Nonetheless, the police spent some time seeking assurance that I would let them handle it. I agreed—their logic prevailed—and Officer Houseman set off to call the local police in Winchester, Virginia, to get ahead of these goons. After all, we knew where they were headed, and the telephone was a lot faster than any car.

They may not have been able to locate them as quickly as I'd liked, but with knowledge of their destination, the police could possibly have headed them off at the pass, so to speak. By the time the officer departed, Pat was at my side. He knew what I was going to do and asked to come along. I hesitated, then said no; it was too dangerous and he had to think of Carolyn and the kids. He laughed, then he insisted, stating that Carolyn knew who he was and that she would support his decision to help.

He was right. She was standing in her driveway with a packed bag and two lunch pails filled with food when we arrived together in his truck. After a long hug and a series of be-careful comments, Pat kissed his wife and we sped off in pursuit of the men who had abducted Maura.

The phone rang twice at the Winchester police station, then officer Gantz answered, speaking rather quickly and writing on his pad. He was a short, stout man who always seemed nervous and filled with anxious energy. He thanked officer Houseman, then he set the handpiece in its cradle. Gantz said nothing; he just rose to his feet and took the doodled images he had scribbled to the trash bin. Then, he continued on with his day. Ray Vitale's cousin was not in the least bit upset by a call from the Scranton Police; he just smiled to himself as he stepped out the door and headed to lunch. Gantz met with Paul Lennox, one of Vitale's boys, and shared the news of the phone call as a piece of pertinent information that he thought his cousin Ray should know about. He insisted that no one else knew a thing and that he would keep it that way. Lennox paid for their lunch, then he returned to Vitale with the information.

The roads were in poor condition, dusty and heavily-rutted, making a trip of under 240 miles a journey. I prayed silently all the way to Virginia for the well-being of my wife. My mind stayed fixed on her. I wished for a way to know she was alright. My only assurance of her health was the knowledge that Vitale wanted to make me suffer and kill me as well. He knew that I would walk right into his waiting gun, trying to save my wife. I knew he would keep her alive, at least until he had the opportunity to exact his revenge and watch as we both suffered at his hand. In some strange way, I sought comfort in that terrible thought. Her life would be spared until we could be together.

Chapter 20

Pat and I drove straight through for 18 hours, arriving in Winchester, Virginia late on Saturday afternoon. We were covered with dust and grime and in need of some rest. I wanted desperately to rush to Maura's side, but as Pat pointed out, we couldn't just stroll into town announcing our arrival. Our desire to go unnoticed drove our decision to utilize the cover of darkness and we set up camp in the woods on the northern side of town. Exhausted from our drive, I rested my eyes in the back of Pat's pickup.

As night fell, we broke camp and headed to Mary's house. Mary, the woman whose husband and child had died at the hands of Vitale's goons, was surprised to see us walking through her yard in the darkness—so surprised, in fact, that a shotgun blast fired into the air, followed by a vicious threat to the hoodlums approaching her home, was the greeting we received and the greeting we deserved.

She heard me plead with her in a whispered tone, as if the shotgun had not already awoken her sleeping family.

"Michael, is that you?" were the words that came from her dangerous-looking silhouette.

A shotgun glimmering in the moonlight is quite dangerous-looking. When I identified myself, the shotgun lowered and the wife of my old friend hurried Pat and me into the kitchen of her home. Pie and coffee were what she offered us first; the note from Vitale's boys was the next gift from my friend. Evidently, my attempt to retrieve my wife was in his plan. I knew this, but when Mary handed me that note, my mind went back to a statement Vitale had made to Maura when she and I had first started dating. Vitale made it abundantly clear that he was not happy with her for not giving him another chance. I believe his exact quote was, "It might not be this week, or this month, or this year, but I have two graves dug for you and the fly boy in the woods. When the time comes, your bodies will fill them."

It scared her at the time, and it terrified me to think of that now, as he held my wife hostage. Again, though, I knew he was waiting to see me suffer as my wife died at his hand before putting me in the grave next to her. The note simply read, "Monday, noon, McAfee Knob, no cops." We now had a time and a place for this showdown of his, but if I just strolled in there expecting to reason with the man or relying upon his mercy, it wouldn't be a showdown at all—just an execution. I knew he was dangerous and supported by an army of goons. I had to outsmart them. Pat and I had to outsmart them all, because our lives depended on it.

The next morning, I woke to the smell of coffee and the tempting waft of pancakes. Pat was already downstairs with Mary. I descended the last set of stairs and said good morning as I pulled out a chair and sat at the table. Pat and I discussed the idea of a preemptive strike, kind of a sneak attack to take the goons and their leader by surprise. We needed information, though; we needed to know exactly where Maura was and what the best way in and out was as we returned her to safety.

Pat had flown several missions in World War I, and I did still have my old biplane at the local airport. I thought a little recon would be a good idea. The weather was perfect. The only problem was that Vitale and his boys knew my airplane. Mary came up with the solution. She took Pat down to the airport and introduced him to an old pilot friend of Tony's. I remained behind to keep out of sight and to add to the story that Pat and Ralph, Mary's pilot friend, were old war buddies. Ralph was as tall as Pat with thick, wavy hair and a bushy mustache. The six-foot-four duo stuck out a bit, but their story was convincing. They actually knew a few of the same guys from Ralph's squadron. A marine himself, Ralph agreed to help and to keep quiet about what was going on.

Within the hour of Mary leaving the house, Pat and Ralph were airborne to scope out Ray Vitale's fortress from high above. Maura heard the plane going back and forth over the mountaintop, so she claimed she needed to use the ladies room, which was an outhouse. Pat spotted her as she crossed the field, confirming that she was OK, at least for the moment. They used the map and a few more passes to mark the outposts of Vitale's men using the cover of towing a banner that advertised plane rides at the upcoming fair. Ray's boys never suspected a thing.

Pat returned with the good news that Maura was fine. She was, in fact, at Vitale's cabin, and the goons were all stationed along the three established paths to the top of the mountain. It was time to put it all together in a plan and step into action. We knew the location of the Sentinels, but we didn't know their schedule. If we could get into position and watch them for a while, we could possibly minimize our exposure and the amount of time outmanned and outgunned.

We each borrowed a pistol and a rifle from Tony's collection. We cleaned and prepped them and took several dozen rounds of ammunition. We also took enough provisions for the night and stuffed everything into a set of army surplus backpacks that Mary's boys used to play with. When night fell, we hiked to the bottom of the mountain and started to climb into the darkened woods, far from any of the established trailheads and the goons that guarded them.

In their arrogance, the men at each of the established checkpoints along the trails had started a relatively large evening bonfire, which made it easy for us to locate and avoid them. Pat and I tracked halfway up the mountain and set up a small tent each; no fire for us. I wanted to figure out what time they changed shifts so we could let the new guys re-establish themselves and the old crew dissipate before we made our move. Pat stayed behind to minimize the noise of our movements, and I snuck slowly through the woods toward the ledge that overlooked the bonfire on Bryson Trail.

The blaze lit up everything for 50 yards. From my perch, I observed the two thugs half in the bag as they sat on a set of tree stumps outside of their tents. They kept toasting each other back and forth, sounding more and more ridiculous with every shot they took. Then the short, fat guy stood up and commanded his buddy to stay awake as he was going to nap for his two hours, and then they would switch.

At first, I thought this might be a good time to take them out, but then Stumpy spoke up again, saying they would alternate watch until the replacements arrived at 8:00am. I didn't want to risk a struggle with the night shift, only to have to battle the replacements in the morning. I decided to wait and stick to our plan. Now that I had the information I needed, I worked my way back to camp and shared the intelligence I gathered with Pat.

I attempted everything possible to calm my racing mind. My wife, the love of my life, was in the hands of an evil man that was intent on killing her. I gave up on the idea of sleep as I laid there with my head propped up in my tent, gazing off at the night sky through the window flap, listening to my friend breathe rhythmically from his little dwelling next door. Pat never seemed to flinch at all, ever. No matter how crazy life got, Pat just pressed on through. That night, he slept in peace as I tossed and turned until exhaustion finally overwhelmed me at about 3:00am and I restlessly drifted away.

The sun rose that morning around five, and we rose with it. Without much to do until that shift change, Pat and I sat up eating muffins Mary had prepared for us and drinking hot coffee from a thermos. Around 7:30 or so, we broke camp and started to work our way back to the overlook. We were in place and remained as still as possible as we watched their changing of the guard. Stumpy and his friend grumbled something to the new crew before heading off up the trail on horseback.

Two versus two seemed like the best odds I'd be seeing all day, and they were. Pat worked his way north up the ridge that ran along the trail, and I worked my way south. As planned, at exactly 9:00am, Pat repelled from the northern rocks, out of sight of the Sentinels. At the same time, south of their encampment, I repelled to the trail myself and started a slow walk toward Vitale's men. Meanwhile, Pat crossed the trail and quietly worked his way toward their flank through the tree line, providing just a little element of surprise to help us out.

The shorter of the two men stood as I approached. I just kept walking slowly in his direction as he crushed his cigarette beneath his boot. When we were standing face-to-face, he opened his coat to show me what he had to show me. I had figured as much. He pointed upward, and I rose my hands so he could frisk me.

"A little early," he said as he checked for weapons.

"Yeah," I replied. "I couldn't sleep."

He just smirked as if to inform me that sleep would no longer be a concern for me.

Then, he looked down at my feet.

"The boots," he said. "Everybody thinks they're tricky hiding something in their boots".

As I bent down toward my boots, Pat made his move. He lit the flare and threw it with all his might. The seated goon fell over backwards as the flare blasted just about an inch from his nose, landing in the tent and setting it on fire. Simultaneously, I grabbed the knife from my boot and jammed it through the instep of my escort, whose head had turned to try to grasp how quickly his surroundings were changing.

As his body bent over in a desperate reaction to remove the knife, I spun around, pouring every ounce of my body weight into his jaw via a spinning hammer fist.
He fell over, unconscious, still kneeling on the leg attached to my Bowie knife When I retrieved my knife, he fell to the side.

Goon number two never stood a chance. By the time he realized what had happened, Pat was sitting on his chest with his knife across the man's throat like Rambo. He didn't so much as flinch when Pat removed his gun and tossed it to me, then took his shirt and hat. We tied the hands of the two men and gagged them, then dragged them into the woods and tied them to two separate trees with their arms behind them, facing away from each other. Pat poured their water jugs on the remains of the little tent fire he'd caused, and we walked north to claim their horses for our own. As we rode away, you couldn't hear a sound from the semi-safari-outfitted gentlemen struggling in the distant woods.

After Pisgah Ridge, the trail became sporadically visible to anyone on McAfee Knob or coming down from Vitale's cabin. Pat and I found a nice clearing lined with trees just off the main trail and just prior to Pisgah Ridge. There, we tied the horse I was riding to a tree and fed him some carrots from his saddlebag. After securing my horse, Pat loosely tied my hands behind my back and we headed back to the trail as captor and captive. Pat rode aboard his trusty steed as I struggled amongst the rocks in the heat of the sun-drenched trail in an effort to make all things appear as they should when we ran into Vitale's next line of defense.

I knew the trail ran north and south with Vitale's cabin just off the main branch, about three miles from our position. After just under a half hour of hiking, the trail became a wooded path. Twenty minutes later, we came upon McAfee knob. Two men were waiting for us as we stepped out from the tree-lined trail onto the large rock ledge. From across the rocks, the taller man motioned to his partner, who then jumped on his horse and headed back to the cabin to tell of our arrival.

The tall man was, in fact, the packless hiker that Maura and I had encountered on the day we had gotten engaged. I remembered his face, with a scar beneath his right eye. That face seemed to react to his every thought; he would not have been a good poker player. The look on his face as Pat dismounted was indicative of him realizing the rider was not one of his men.

Before he could open his mouth, though, Pat hit him so hard that his knees buckled. As he was falling, Pat hit him with the butt of his pistol, and the man fell silent. Pat tied

Scarface with the rope from the horse's saddle, then he cut the man's shirt and made him a personalized gag. Then he literally ditched the thug in the gully on the side of the trail.

I walked to the edge of the knob. Looking down, I saw the two rectangular ditches. I guess Vitale's plan was to do away with Maura and me, then toss us over the ridge and send a few of his boys to tidy things up. Maybe they would even cover it all with some fallen leaves. Our bodies would never have been discovered. It was on one hand chilling to see the graves in reality, but on the other hand, the sight of those rectangular trenches instilled in me a sense of determination that was unlike anything I had ever felt before. I was not going to let anything happen to my wife.

No way in hell was he going to get away with this.
My old friend Aman, a gentleman of Indian descent, once said, "If you mess with me, karma will get you. If you mess with my family, I'm karma." I no longer wanted to just defend myself. I wanted to hunt that bastard down and make him pay for his attacks on the woman I love. He may have put her through hell, but I was on a mission to send that

arrogant son-of-a-bitch to a permanent residence amongst the fire and brimstone.

McAfee Knob was a large clearing of stone along the ridge that would in later years be a celebrated section of the Appalachian Trail. The knob itself is an outcropping of stone that overlooks the valley below with an on-top-of-the-world type of view that would become the backdrop for millions of photos over years to come. It was spectacular. Mcafee Knob was the place that Maura and I had gotten engaged, and now it stood the very real chance of being our headstone, so to speak, if we were to be buried in the graves below as Vitale had planned.

Chapter 21

The lone horseman approached Vitale's cabin, riding at full sprint. Then, he pulled hard on the reins and dismounted from the side as the horse came to a stop in pain, rearing up just slightly.

"Jimmy brought him up, all tied nice and neat," the horseman said to the two men sitting on the porch. "He and Steve are with him, waiting at the knob."

"I'll meet you at the stable," said one man, standing and approaching the rider. "Start saddling the horses."

He turned and followed the other man inside. They informed Vitale, who just nodded his head and took another shot of whiskey. Maura was tied to the living room chair, her head hanging in silence. Her wrists were red and raw, but other than that, she had not suffered at the hands of her captors. One thug untied her then promptly cuffed her hands behind her back.

They headed out the back door toward the stable. When Vitale finally joined them, Maura was already mounted on the smallest of five horses. Vitale put his left foot in the stirrup, then he threw his right leg over his horse. He looked down at Maura and touched her cheek as she pulled away.

"Pity," he said. "Such a pretty girl. Such a waste of beauty."

She shrugged back and nearly lost her balance as the group of horses moved forward in unison. Little John pulled gently on the reins of her horse and laughed out loud. They rode in a diamond formation, surrounding Vitale for his protection. The ride from the cabin to McAfee Knob was brief; no one really spoke. The trail ended abruptly and opened onto the rocks. We were soon in their sight as they rounded the corner.

Chapter 22

I was sitting on a rock with my hands behind my back. Pat lorded over me, fully in character, with a loaded gun to my head as they rounded the corner into the clearing from the north. They crossed the rocks and dismounted. Maura, ever the fighter, kicked little John, a giant of a man, right in his smirking mouth as he tried to touch her breast while helping her dismount. Then she dropped to the ground, catching her balance with the bend of her knee. When little John raised his hand to hit her, Vitale just grabbed it from behind and pushed him aside.

Grabbing Maura's upper arm, Vitale pushed her to Donny, his lead henchman, then he stepped in front of me.

"Enough bull…," said Vitale, his profanity interrupted.

Before Ray Vitale could finish speaking, I felt the gun move from the back of my head. One of the two goons behind

Donny realized that Pat was not who he seemed, and he started to reach for his gun. His partner followed suit, but before they could move, Pat put a bullet squarely in each of their heads. As soon as I had felt the gun removed from my head, I let the loosely-tied ropes fall from my hands and lunged toward Vitale. Donny instinctively pushed Maura aside and tried to help his boss, but Maura wasn't done.

She jumped up in the air and pushed her legs between her handcuffed arms. Still cuffed, she grabbed Donny from behind, choking him with the chain of the cuffs. I spun away from Vitale and grabbed Donny by the hair on the back of his head, and my palm smashed his jaw. In one smooth motion, I snapped Donny's neck. As Donny fell, Maura let go and his lifeless body dropped from the cliff.

Just then, I felt the steel of a gun barrel on the back of my head and heard Vitale yelling to Pat to drop his gun. Pat obliged, then Vitale promptly and momentarily removed the gun from my head to take a casual shot in Pat's direction, hitting him in the thigh.

"I'll deal with you later," he said smugly.

Vitale spun me around, regaining control of the situation as Maura and I were in front of him and Pat was injured a safe distance away. He motioned the gun at us, then he spoke bluntly to Maura.

"You might as well jump; I'm only going to shoot you otherwise," Vitale remarked casually. "He'll be right behind you. I just want to watch him endure the pain of losing you before I send him to his death."

The knob where we stood jutted out from the mountain where, 400 feet below, our graves were already dug. Maura and the cliff were off to my left. Vitale stood in front of me, pointing the gun. He started to raise his voice.

"You caused all of this. Now jump, you bitch!" he screamed into her face.

The gun was pointed at me, holding me at bay as his anger rose. I knew it was time for a last-ditch effort. My hands were raised in the traditional surrendering fashion, but before I could even think about what to do, an old move from my Tang Soo Do class erupted from my body on pure instinct. In a split second, I flung my hands towards the gun, each with the thumb tucked to the side. The striking motion was known as a ridge hand. My right hand struck Vitale's wrist as my left hand simultaneously smashed the back of his hand and his gun went flying. It hit a rock 15 feet away, discharging a cartridge, then it tumbled into the grass.

I took advantage of his surprise. I grabbed his wrist with my hand, pulling it toward me, as my left elbow plowed forward to break his arm. It was as though it was out of my control; one fluid motion. The motion did not stop there. I grabbed Vitale by the hair and side-kicked his knee from behind, driving his kneecap into the stone and bringing his head to the level of my chest. Then, as the rage began to peak inside me, I snapped his head backwards, exposing his throat, and I grabbed his windpipe with my right hand, squeezing it for all it was worth.

With sweat pouring from my brow, I actually thought of letting him go. This had all gotten too out of hand. I never wanted to kill a man, and this would be the second time in ten minutes. As he gasped for air, strewn across my knee, I paused and contemplated getting him help. Then, my mind filled with the history of all that he had done: little Emma, Tony, kidnapping Maura. The constant threat that he posed to our lives. I heard a gun discharge from my right side. Thinking it was one of his men intent on stopping me, I grasped his throat once more. My inner rage won out. When I rose to my feet, his last few gasps left his body as it fell those 400 feet from the ridge right into one of the graves he had dug for my wife and me.

Maura pulled me back, preventing his weight from taking me with him. We stood united, hugging one another, and then we kissed briefly. We looked toward Pat. In excruciating pain from his wound, he had dragged his body into the grass, retrieving Vitale's gun. The gunshot I'd heard was from Pat, taking out the last of Vitale's men. One last goon had descended the trail and was standing behind a rock with a rifle pointed at me. Pat had stopped him before he had the chance to fire.

Maura and I helped to dress the wound on Pat's leg. The bullet had gone through and wouldn't need to be removed. That was a relief. I feared the remaining goons would be on their way, heading in the direction of the gunshots. When we got Pat standing, the three of us started down the trail. Instead of Vitale's thugs, we met the sheriff. Our friend Mary had sent a whole battalion in our direction.

We spent another week in town with Mary. The sheriff's office was a daily stop; the questions seemed endless. When all was said and done, every goon had indeed put forth sufficient threat, and the whole mess was considered an act of self-defense. Pat, Maura and myself were free to go. We escorted Pat to the train where he met Carolyn, and they traveled home together. Maura and I said our goodbyes to Mary and to Maura's aunt and uncle at the airport. It was both a sad and joyous time, but in the future, our visits would be regular. With the threat removed, we shared some spectacular holidays with Uncle Jackie and Aunt Joan over the years.

With Maura on board, Uncle Jackie propped the airplane for me. The little engine of my old biplane chugged gently to life, and we waved as we taxied to the far end of the airfield. I looked forward at her flowing, strawberry-blonde ponytail coming from beneath her flying cap, then down at the picture in my cockpit, and I smiled. Although I couldn't see her face, I knew she was smiling too.

As I pushed the throttle to the firewall, the tailskid raised first. Then, with the gentlest of back pressure on the control stick, the pristine little Eaglerock lifted us into the sky together. We rose away from the ground that morning, free at last, into a life filled with friends, family and more adventure than any one couple deserved. It was a terribly rocky start for us, but when you are that madly in love, you find a way to get through.

We did more than just get through. Every year brought us into a new challenge, a new adventure, a new blessing. After what we had lived through in order to be together, we were forever grateful for the many blessings that life had bestowed upon us.

So there you have it, the story of how Maura and I became husband and wife. Quite a story, I know. If you believe in one thing, believe in this: true love is out there. I'm referring to the person that you just can't live without; the one who turns your world upside down. That person, the best friend you'll ever have, the love of your life, that take-your-breath-away soulmate, does exist. For those of us who are lucky enough to have found that special someone, we should cherish them. We should be grateful for them every day, for life is short, but a good life has few regrets. Maura and I have so very few regrets. God bless.

Epilogue

There it all is, in my grandfather's words: a spectacular tale of time travel, love, romance, chivalry, gangsters, family and friends. All put together, I think it does show merit as some type of book. Sadly, the night he placed this journal in my hands, Michael Joseph Nevin passed away. He had a heart attack in his home just after he'd spread the embers from his evening fire and started toward the stairs.

Maybe he was chasing another apparition of Maura. I know how he would have worded it. He would have said that he simply died of a broken heart. As to his journal, I never knew for sure where in these tales of his the truth really lied. On one hand, I would like to know;

on the other, I like the story just as it is. If you'd known my grandfather and the passion of his tales, you would know that the spirit and steadfast love his writing has put forth always shined through in his everyday life. He was definitely that man, the man of honor and courage that he wrote about.

Maybe it's all true. In the spirit of belief, I find myself with one more mission to honor my grandpa. I wrote this note, you see, it's just a handwritten note in big letters with a simple statement:

Open your mind,

trust your heart.

His address on this date, August 4, 1993, was in that journal. Just on the odd chance that time travel and soulmates have a place within this universe, I'm going to be sure that this note makes it to the front door of that address.

An homage to my grandfather and his wild tales? Yes, to say the least, but maybe it has something to do with bringing things full-circle. You know what I mean.

Sincerely,

Christopher Nevin

August 4, 1993

Author's Note

I want to thank my wife Judi for being the love of my life and my inspiration and for always supporting my desire to be a writer. I would like to take a moment and thank my son Christopher Rencavage, the filmmaker, for some wonderful ideas that truly enhanced this book and for his continuous support of my writing. I want to thank Aunt Joan and Uncle Jackie for showing us what a soulmate really is. Thank you to my friend Bill Ferri of Ferri's Pizza in Moscow, PA, where he keeps what I believe is the largest personal collection of mining memorabilia in the United States. Thank you, Billy, for sharing your time and insights. I want to thank all of our family and friends for their love and support, especially those who gave their time and shared their opinions for the betterment of this book. The beta readers hold a special spot in my heart. Very important to any book is professional editing: a thanks goes out to my editors, Carlene Majorino, who helped me to get moving again and bring this book to a level of completion that allowed for it to be submitted for publication. Another thanks to Robert Charette, who helped with the very first edit of this work. These two very talented young professional writers are a blessing to have in my life. Also, a special thanks to Stuart Grimm, my good friend and beta reader, who gifted me the Brazilian cherry handmade inkpen that wrote the first draft of this novel. One final thanks to the Eagles Mere Air museum for their time and efforts and the use of their beautiful aircraft.

About the Author

Mike Rencavage is a professional aviator with thirty years of flying experience; having held positions as a flight instructor and pilot for both general aviation and the airlines. He is currently a corporate pilot for Flexjet LLC out of Cleveland, Ohio. Flexjet is consider the Nation's premier aviation fractional ownership company. He is the father of two amazing young men Michael K (Mikey) Rencavage and Christopher Joseph Rencavage. His blended family is completed with his wife Judi and her two sons Patrick and Taylor. He was born and raised in Scranton, Pennsylvania and now resides in Dallas, Pa.

Mike has authored three books and been published several times in magazines and journals in the fields of aviation and rehabilitation engineering.(A former career path) He loves family and friends and all things aviation. He and his wife Judi are avid motorcyclists and enjoy hiking on the great trails throughout Pennsylvania, Virginia, West Virginia and the Carolinas.

Contact me at: mikethewriter53@gmail.com

Made in the USA
Middletown, DE
29 April 2023